PRAISE FOR NATHALIE SARRAUTE

"Sarraute . . . does not develop a plot. She repeats, and constantly modifies, analyses of a small number of episodes. . . . This technique does not exhaust human reality, or sterilize it, but enriches it. The complexity of feelings and reactions it reveals is extraordinary, and it is also true: this is the way things are, and no other technique would be (or at least has shown itself to be) so capable of rendering reality at this level."

—*Saturday Review*

"The best thing about Nathalie Sarraute is her stumbling, groping style, with its honesty and numerous misgivings, a style that approaches the object with reverent precautions, withdraws from it suddenly out of a sort of modesty, or through timidity before its complexity, then, when all is said and done, suddenly presents us with the drooling monster, almost without having touched it, through the magic of an image."

—Jean-Paul Sartre

"Nathalie Sarraute's use of metaphor is abundant and distinctive, providing a texture so rich and complex as to belie the simplicity of the novel's structure."

—*New York Times Book Review*

"Mme. Sarraute has a ruthless and dramatic notion of the quest of Reality."

—V. S. Pritchett

"There are few living writers I admire more than Nathalie Sarraute. Every sentence that she writes is priceless. The first to do so since Proust, she has introduced something new."

—Claude Mauriac

"The technique consists of a trivial incident, but the result is a shrewd, ultimately moving analysis of the rift between parents and children, extended to the rift between present and past."

—*Atlantic Monthly*

"An intense and curious book which plunges the reader into reality both familiar—even rat ed."

Times

DO YOU HEAR THEM?

TRANSLATION BY MARIA JOLAS

Nathalie Sarraute

DALKEY ARCHIVE PRESS

Originally published in French as *Vous les entendez?* by Éditions Gallimard, 1972
Originally published in English by George Braziller, Inc., 1973

Library of Congress Cataloging-in-Publication Data

Sarraute, Nathalie, 1900-99.
  [Vous les entendez? English]
  Do you hear them? / Nathalie Sarraute ; translated by Maria Jolas.
    p. cm.
  ISBN 1-56478-329-4 (alk. paper)
    I. Jolas, M. II. Title

PQ2637.A783V613 2004
843'.914—dc21

                                           2003055103

Partially funded by grants from the National Endowment for the Arts, a federal agency,
and the Illinois Arts council, a state agency.

Dalkey Archive Press books are published by the Center for Book Culture, a nonprofit organization,
located at Milner Library, Illinois State University.

www.centerforbookculture.org

Printed on permanent/durable acid-free paper and bound in the United States of America.

FOR MY OLD AND DEAR FRIEND,
MARIA JOLAS

Do You
Hear Them?

Suddenly he interrupts himself, raises his hand, his forefinger in the air, he listens... Do you hear them?... a gentle melancholy mellows his features... They're light-hearted, eh? They're enjoying themselves... After all, that goes with their age... We, too, used to have fits of laughter like that... we couldn't stop...

—Yes, that's true... He feels his own lips stretching, a good-natured smile wrinkles his cheeks, gives his mouth a toothless look... that's quite true, we were like them... It doesn't take much, does it? to make them laugh... Yes, they are light-hearted.

Both heads are raised, they listen... Yes, young laughter. Fresh laughter. Carefree laughter. Silvery laughter. Tiny bells. Tiny drops. Fountains. Gentle water-falls. Twittering of birds... They're dusting their wings, frisking about... As soon as they were by themselves they forgot us.

Yes, clear, transparent laughter... The kind of childlike, charming laughter that comes through the doors of parlors to which the ladies have retired after dinner... Loose-fitting chintz covers in faded shades. Sweet-peas in the old vases. Coals glowing, logs burning bright in the fireplaces... Their innocent, pert slightly mischievous laughter comes in peals... Dimples, pinkness, blondness, roundness, long dresses of tulle, of white lace, of English embroidery, moiré belts, flowers in their hair and on their bosoms... the pure notes of their crystalline laughter come in ripples... They are enjoying themselves... Do you hear them?

The gentlemen seated around the table tap their well-seasoned old pipes, sip their brandy... So many care-free childhoods have deposited here their thicknesses of security, of serene candor. They are talking together in low, slow voices, they grow silent a second to listen...

Yes, they are light-hearted, that goes with their age. Goodness only knows what makes them laugh... nothing, absolutely nothing, nothing they could tell, so little is needed, the silliest things, just any old word and it starts up—impossible to stop, it can't be helped.

And yet they are tired... so weary... the day had been a long one, the country air, exercise... They raise their hands to their heads, they tap their mouths which discreet yawns have half-opened, they rise at a signal exchanged between them... A scarcely perceptible signal... No, no signal... Yes, why not? The moment has come, hasn't it, when it is not impolite to take leave? ...and they go upstairs... The old friend who came in for a neighborly chat after dinner follows them with his placid gaze.

Now they are alone, seated opposite each other. On the low table, the bottles and glasses have been moved aside to make room for the heavy animal of rough stone that the friend has taken from the mantelpiece, carried cautiously and set down there, between them. His gaze, his hand, caress with respect, with fondness, its flanks, its back, its thick snout...

What issues from there, what emanates, radiates, flows, penetrates them, filters all through them, what fills them, dilates them, uplifts them... makes a sort of void around them in which they are floating, in which they let themselves be borne along... no word can describe... But they have no need of words, they don't want any, they know that above all no word should be allowed to approach it, touch it, they must see to it that the carefully chosen, highly selective words, decent, unobtrusive words, be held at a respectful distance: Really, you've got there a splendid specimen... Yes, there do occur such breaks, such strokes of luck... Once, I remember, I was on mission in Cambodia and, at a little junkdealer's... at first I thought... and then, you know, when I looked at it more closely...

Now the laughter has stopped. After all, they had to go to bed. You can't keep on babbling all night long... and about what? Is it possible to imagine such piffle, such emptly twaddle... But it's finished, they have separated, each one has shut the door of his room, they have finally stopped talking... there's nothing more... and the air would seem to have grown lighter, there's a sensation of release, of freedom, of uncon-cern... now he stretches out his hand and lays it on the rough stone... It's true, it has a kind of denseness... I'm glad that you too... There are people who think...

And there it is starting up again... softly... in light outbursts... and brief fits and starts... it comes through the closed door, it insinuates itself... The other, opposite, goes on calmly talking... Perhaps he doesn't notice it any longer? Or perhaps he hears it the way we hear the hum of flies, the stridulation of crick-ets... It stops... Starts again... Doesn't it really sound as though someone were prudently drilling?...

But here we are protected. What powerful tools would one not need to perforate, to crack these thick walls behind which they have taken shelter, with it set there between them... A funny animal, isn't it? His hand feels its contours, flatters its heavy flanks... I wonder what it is... perhaps a puma, and yet... no, it's not like anything... Look at those paws and those enormous ears shaped like sea-shells... it's more likely a mythological animal... a religious object... nobody has ever been able to tell me...

Silvery laughter. Crystalline laughter. A bit too much? A bit like theatrical laughter? No, perhaps

4

not... yes, all the same, it looks as though it were possible to detect... Not so, there's a slight explosion, the kind that can't be held in... Oh, be quiet, stop, you'll be the death of me, I can't bear it, they can hear us... But look at him... ha, ha, do look, he's a scream... Just anything will do for them... Nothing, less than nothing... Nonsense—childishness...

Nothing that could touch us and make us waver, we who are so sturdy and erect, so well-planted... We who grew up amid sweet-peas, pots of geraniums and impatiens, flowered percales, white cretonnes, faithful old servants, cooks whose faces shone with kindliness, grandmothers in lace caps, giving a sip of wine to newly-hatched chicks...

Not at all, no need of sweet-peas, of chicks, of grandmothers. Take just anybody, search the wide world over, you won't find anyone among the least sheltered, the most neglected, the most disquiet, distrustful, trembling, who could... who could or would?... Could or would?... no matter... who could or would see in this laughter... But how could he? Who, unless he had been prepared... who, unless he had been trained, could have... when with his air of peaceful self-assurance the old friend approached the mantelpiece, stretched out his hand and caressed... who could have perceived the threat, the danger, the commotion, the disorderly flight, the appeals, the entreaties... No, not that, don't do that, don't touch it... not now, not before them, not as long as they are there, not while they are watching... when he advanced... like a powerful ice-breaker, opening, cleaving, shattering enormous blocks... everything scattered... when he cautiously lifted, transported and set down there in their midst, while they looked on saying nothing... and then quietly took his stand at a certain distance and contemplated, smacking his lips... this animal... really magnificent... A splendid specimen. Where did you have such luck?... —No, no, it was not me. It was at my father's... I don't know where my father... I myself, you know, am not a collector. I would even say the contrary... As if that could deceive them, as if this cowardly disavowal, this deception which they are observing amusedly, could appease them, could prevent what is going to happen now, inevitable, foreseeable in its minutest details like the application of a sentence carried out with rigorous precision by executioners who are insensitive to repentance, to the condemned man's cries.

From this moment on it was all there, concentrated in that second... How do you mean all? Nothing occurred. They rose, they politely took leave, they were so tired... and now, as can happen, alone again they revived, they relaxed and they're enjoying themselves... they need so little... for them just anything suffices... How do you mean anything? Oh, any kind of nonsense, making faces, imitations... nobody knows better than that little wag, a regular little clown, how to stick his tongue under his upper lip, which is very long, squint his eyes, bend his back, and one hand scratching under his arm, imitate a monkey... That makes them die laughing every time... Anything will do for them, isn't that so? Why look for problems where none exist? They're young, they're light-hearted...

That the irascible old fogey should suddenly rise under the surprised eyes of his friend who was peace-fully sipping his cup of coffee, his glass of cassis, that he should suddenly break all the rules of propriety, that he should go upstairs, knock on the door, open it in a fury, that he should go in... What on earth is the matter for you to be laughing like this? It gets to be unbearable, finally... and they're going to stop, cower in corners, scared to death, startled nymphs caught unawares by a satyr, little pink pigs dancing when all of a sudden, howling, his great teeth bared, in comes the big bad wolf, chickens that take refuge on the top beams of the hen-house into which has just entered the crafty, cruel fox. The wicked ogre, the spoilsport, the cop... What's wrong now? What have we done now? We couldn't leave? It's because we dawdled around a bit here, too tired to go to bed? How did he hear us? We were laughing so softly... But he's always there watch-ing everything we do, repressing the slightest impulse, the slightest sign of carefreeness, of freedom, always examining, measuring, judging. Didn't we show the respect we should have? Didn't we approach the sacred object as though we were looking at it for the first time? Didn't I go so far, I too, as to lay my

7

hand... you saw me? —reverently... But that's not enough. After that, probably, we should have maintained a religious silence, gone up to bed steeped in devotion... No, not go to bed, what was I thinking about? What savagery! What a sacrilege! We should have stayed there without being able to pull ourselves away, glued there, listening until dawn without feeling any fatigue... Wouldn't that wake the dead?

That's not true, they're mistaken, they're wrong, he's not a supervisor, not a cop... May they pardon him, they who are so pure, they who are innocent, they who are, he wants to believe it, he does believe it, they who are reserved—he is less so than they are—they who do not like to show their feelings, they who perhaps have genuine respect for these "values"... they should excuse this awful word, he taught it to them, he blushes for it... He would be happy now if he could stay with them a bit, he's bored down there, away from them... Why did they leave him?... Couldn't I join you? You know, I'm like the Irishman, you heard this story? Seeing some people quarreling, he went up to them and said: Can I join in? Or is it a private quarrel?... Ha, ha, ha, they burst out laughing... Oh that is funny, I didn't know that one... —What were you talking about while I, down there... I don't believe he'll ever leave... You saw how he looked at me when I said that I was nothing of a collector?

Why, of course, they had seen, they had heard, they had taken in... fully... There's not a tremor in him, however slight, that they don't sense right away, taught, drilled by him as they are, possessing all the most de-

tailed maps, real ordnance maps, gifts from him, constantly being brought up to date under his guidance,
of this terrain which they are now occupying in complete security... the sharp peals of their laughter slip
into every coil, permeate every recess...

And then stop...

They wait a bit... they want to reassure him, let
him believe that it's over, that the punishment has
lasted long enough, that upstairs they have decided he
has had his share... they're enjoying his relief, poor
thing, he doesn't know that he's losing nothing by
waiting, that the time will soon come when, it can't be
helped, it'll have to begin again...

And yet so little, a single movement can crush them,
not even crush, efface them with one stroke without
leaving a single trace—not a single spirt, not a stain...
all that is needed is to lean across the table toward the
innocent creature sitting peacefully on the other side,
tapping with the bent-up end of his thumb on the bowl
of the pipe he is holding in his big pudgy hand, it's
enough to lean toward him, to let oneself go, to un-
bosom oneself, to let oneself fill up with those words
he lets fall with such quiet assurance... without realiz-
ing their effect... How could he, who is so protected,
so confident, he who has never suspected the existence
of secret pacts, of demons, of witchery, evil spells,
voodoo... And how this ignorance, this ingenuousness
increases more than ever the exorcising power of the
words that he articulates clearly, with a dignified,

worthy drawl: Yes, yes, sometimes you do have such strokes of luck... really undreamed of. I remember, at that time, I was on mission in Cambodia... and one day, quite by chance, in a rather squalid sort of little shop, the kind in which you least expect to find... filled with a hodgepodge... all kinds of cheap things, the kind that are mass-produced for foreigners..., it was full of shoddy buddhas, stuffed birds... I don't know what impelled me to go in... there are days when you have sort of premonitions... I picked up the corner of a rug, the pattern looked amusing to me... and there... I couldn't believe my eyes... a real little marvel... but you've seen it at my place... —The little dancing girl? —Yes. That's it. The shopkeeper hadn't the vaguest suspicion... Of course I didn't let on anything... And you know, that's not out of greed... He nods his head vigorously... Yes I know. Obviously there's no question of that. It's something else.

Yes, he knows, he understands... It's to be alone, alone to know, alone to discover. It's to create, to confer life a second time. To snatch from death, from decay, from depreciation, to press against one's breast and, refraining from running, bring it back home, shut oneself in with it... alone together... no one should disturb us... and taking out his tools, his pure wool rags, pure linen rags, his emery-boards, his chamois-skins, his paint-brushes, his other brushes, his varnish removers, his oils, his waxes, his bottles of varnish, scratch, coat, wait, calculate, hope, despair, persist, scrape again, rub, as though his own life depended on it... stopping, worn out, starting again, forgetting to

10

eat, to sleep... until finally... —Ah, it was still more beautiful than I had hoped. Under the layer of cheap paint, not a particle that's been retouched, not a crack... the wood quite undamaged... of excellent quality... a beauty, but you've seen it... Yes, he has seen it... resplendent, occupying the place of honor, surrounded with consideration, its rights restored... —Yes. I admired it...

But I myself, you understand... I... I must say that I have never been a collector... Never, isn't that so? That they know. That you know, over there? I never have been. I haven't got, you'll grant me this, the temperament for it. It's not my nature... On the contrary... That makes them smile. The contrary of a collector... What clumsiness... the things they make you say when they are there listening to you... But it's true, he's not one. No, that's not where he belongs, not at all. They shouldn't put him there, not in the same bag, not in the same section. That's not his case. They must not shut him up with such as those... They must remember, they couldn't have forgotten it... we laughed over it together... we thought they were so comical, those harmless lunatics prowling about the old-iron market, the flea-market, the stamp-market... it was a scream, he was laughing with them... Not out of tact, not out of politeness... too polite to be honest... No, not at all, no, they shouldn't think that, he had laughed whole-heartedly, it was so funny, ludicrous, they told it with such wit, they described it so

11

well... that fellow at the barracks with the eyeglasses... sweeping the yard... and all at once they saw him stop... he stooped over, holding his glasses against his nose, knelt down... what was it? a little weed... what do you think it was? chickweed probably... he picked it with precaution, with reverence, and came to show it to us... he blew on it to separate the tiny petals... let us admire them... he laid it between two sheets of cigarette paper to dry it and evenings, in the barracks-room, he pasted it in his album...

No, not there, not with that one, not with all those aging children with their ecstatic faces leaning ground-ward, lifted heavenward, picking chickweed, holding out butterfly nets... no, not with them... not with the ones who hunt, nose about, seize upon, bring home, choose between, classify, protect, keep, endlessly accumulate, jealously retain in their possession, at their disposal, to enjoy all alone, to exhibit with pride... No, he's not one of those... on the contrary...

On the contrary. He has nothing of the collector about him... That they know well... Yes, they know it... They know that. By heart. They know that song... every note of it... still the same old tune. Haven't they heard it enough... On the contrary... to know that that belongs to me, you understand... I must say that that tarnishes, as it were, yes, it detracts from the perfection of... my happiness... it alters the serenity, the kind of detachment that I need... anyway, you see...

Of course they see. How could he think that they don't see? Haven't they been trained enough?

12

Haven't they followed enough in his train, with him indifferent to the fatigue of long walks through interminable galleries, suites of immense rooms, indifferent to the exhaustion of remaining standing for hours, in the mournful presence, under the sleepy supervision of museum guards, in the promiscuity of visitors being herded in ceaseless droves, closely gathered about them while being subjected to the throbbing beat, the petrifying infiltration of the comments, the explanations... But he, not sensing all that, unaware, as though in a deep hypnotic sleep, seemed to float detached, to drift far from them, far from himself... while they marked time beside him, waiting in silence for him to come out of his trance... Yes... you see, I must confess that as for me, I prefer... on the contrary...

The friend suddenly leans back, raises his eyebrows and stares at him with a troubled gaze... Indeed! On the contrary... Why? —Oh, I don't know... I expressed myself badly... he is spluttering, he is blushing... Naturally... I understand... but what I mean to say... They are watching, amused, a bit embarrassed for him, his awkward efforts to get out of this hornet's nest, to extricate himself from this quagmire into which he sees that he has absentmindedly stuck his foot... What I mean to say, is that I... well... he's floundering more and more, he's bogged down... I must confess that as for me I prefer...

What? He prefers what? He should admit it. But he doesn't need to admit it. Everyone here knows it. What he prefers is certainty. It's security. It's never having to make an effort, to hunt, to ask himself questions, to take sides, to run risks... He prefers to have everything given him, graciously presented. He likes nothing so much as to come and eat out of your hand... in troughs which others have generously filled with choice victuals that are guaranteed... to be able quietly to guzzle, or delicately to pick at this and that, according to his appetite or to his whim of the moment.

It's that, it's clear, that's what he prefers. But there's more to come. The poor dupe sitting opposite him deserves to be warned. Do you know with whom you're dealing? Do you know that you're faced with an impostor? Yes, this sluggard, this cad, this parasite, passes himself off as a "connoisseur." He has the nerve to do this. How do you mean? What proof? That's just it, there is none. That's his strong point. He doesn't have to give any proof. He *feels* more acutely than anybody else and that will do. Imagine, he has the luck to have within himself an instrument that immediately starts to vibrate, a piece of litmus paper that unfailingly changes color... He can't be wrong, he's like that, you see... Why have proof? Fie on you, he refuses to give any. No proof—it's safer. As you see, even that, that piece of sculpture, he said it himself, he didn't discover it, no, not he, he denies it... He's not a collector... On the contrary.

Their clear, limpid laughter... living water, springs, little brooks running through flowering meadows...

their laughter which he is sullying, muddying, by pouring over it... where did he get all that from? From inside himself, of course. From whom else? Inside himself alone. He is alone. Alone with that inside him... All he asks is to be unburdened of it. They should relieve him of it, those who are listening, their faces beaming with kindly smiles, who are tapping peacefully on their old pipes, one ear cocked, heads raised with a nostalgic, fond expression... Do you hear them? They're enjoying themselves, eh? that goes with their age. They're light-hearted.

Light-hearted. Young. Carefree. Anything makes them laugh. It's just that little tremolo... it seems a bit forced... as though it were put on... the hard, icy notes drum like hailstones... Where did she get that, that second-rate actress's laugh that she's been affecting lately? Everything clings to her, she catches everything, gestures, looks, words, intonations, accents... she's constantly playing a role... shaking her curls, opening her eyes wide, with her baby-face pout, her look of a young bride married against her will to an awful old fogey... who sees him come in all of a sudden fuming, brandishing his gnarled fist, shaking the tassel of his nightcap... a testy old chap whom everything exasperates, who cannot stand games, innocent laughter... jealous, who would believe it? of her younger brothers, of her sisters... but she knows how to take him, he never dares hold out against her when she looks him straight in the eye like that... Look the way he turns round right away, hangs his head, he goes down again sheepishly, contrite, he sits down without saying a word... he abides by the lesson, the punishment, he knows perfectly well that he deserved it... he humbly acquiesces... Yes, you're right. That goes with their age. Yes, it's true, we were like them... They're light-hearted.

It really is astonishing, admirable, the way once that has started it unreels ineluctably with the precision of a wheel in a minutely adjusted clockworks. There's never a skip. One touch is enough, however light... but here nothing can ever be too light... for all the tiny little wheels that interlock exactly with one another to start going... The gaze that the gentle innocent seated opposite him turns all of a sudden... the suddenly attentive gaze that he brings to a halt and lets dwell on the mantelpiece, there, right in the middle... the movement he makes, pulling himself up, chest forward, ready to rise... But what is happening? What's got into him? Why, all of a sudden? And yet it had been there for a long time without his ever... What evil fate is egging him on? What demon is amusing itself by playing this farce?... There, he's standing up... he's not going to do that?... Yes, he is... unconscious as a lunatic walking on the edge of a roof, he advances...

And he himself immediately looks away, turns toward them, standing there motionless, silently watching. Now he begins to rise, he stands up, he goes toward them, his neck stretched forward, a beseeching look... he utters the words that, he hopes, are going to show them that he is asking to take refuge among them, to be accepted in their midst, the passwords that will permit him to change to their side: How was your hike? And the fishing expedition?... lower, lower still, he leans over, he lowers his head, he pats, caresses their dog's back, he gives it his hand to lick, to bite on... Ah, you rascal... ah, you little scamp... But nothing can make them give way... the fuse of the infernal machine has been lighted, it is slowly being consumed... In spite of his fear he succeeds in giving a sideward glance... And he sees the insane man standing in front of the mantelpiece stretch out his hands, pick up the stone animal... carry it toward the low table... make an imperious sign to them which they hasten to obey, dashing forward, pushing aside the bottles and glasses... set it down devoutly, and then step back. Stiffens. Contemplates. As though nothing were wrong. There. Before them... It's more than he has the strength to bear, he hides his face, he encircles their knees with his arms...

But without looking at him they detach him from them, push him away... Behave yourself, after all... One should show courtesy to one's guest, to one's friend... It's rude to interrupt him that way... Listen to what he's saying to you. Do you hear him? He is saying: You have there a splendid specimen. You must answer when you're spoken to. Yes... they're right... he obeys... he sits up, he lifts his head... Yes... his voice is colorless, lifeless... Yes, you think

17

so? and right away, once more, he can't help it, he leans over, he strains toward what is warm, quivering, capering about, toward what he loves as they do, what like them he prefers, good old life that you seize with both hands, that you hug... Ah, nice doggie, come, there's a good dog... he rubs his hand over the silken underbelly, squeezes between his fingers the nice soft paws, their soles warm and rough-grained, as though dried in the sun...

But pitilessly, with a few taps in the back, they call him to order... See here, what kind of behavior is this? How can you be so impolite? Get up, why don't you, go and look... Even we, as you see, we go look, we're setting you an example: Yes. It's very fine. Yes. They nod their heads, as is meet, with a look of gravity... they turn to him: Isn't it fine? Don't you think so? Don't you think that it's really a splendid specimen?... Docilely his gaze follows the direction of theirs, mingles with theirs, and borne along by the same current it flows, spreads out over what is there in the middle of the table: an animal, roughly carved out of a gritty, dirty-gray material... The line of the back too straight... The paws out of proportion... too short?... too widely spread?... But you... you... my beauty... straining, holding out his hands... Oh you... you..., you... in a low voice, gritting his teeth.. Ah, yes, eh? you want to be petted, that's it, eh?... you like that... Down, doggie!... ah you're licking... ah, you're biting...

A little decency, for goodness' sake, a little dignity, a little seriousness. What are these questionable

18

games? What do you think you look like? Really, you shame us. Where do you think you are? Aren't we here among decent people? among cultivated people? Look at us... They crowd around the table... What is it, do you think? From what epoch? Where do you think it comes from? They listen attentively, they nod respectfully.

Their laughter explodes even louder... they've lost control of it... that's natural, that happens when you're tired, or when you've just escaped some danger, in tragic moments, in important circumstances, on solemn occasions, at funerals, weddings, during inauguration, coronation ceremonies... there are people, this is well known, who are suddenly seized with uncontrollable laughter. Just now they are like schoolchildren who have just been let out for recess... They've made such an effort, they've listened so attentively to the lesson, that afterward, this is quite normal, they relax, they erupt... He was funny when he assumed that look of a schoolman in cap and gown... You know he used to be a professor... Of what, ye Gods! I pity his students... Why, of art history, of course, ho, ho...

But how naïve, how stupid to attribute such remarks to them... Nothing of the sort was said... Nothing of the sort was said between themselves... Never... that would be altering entirely the rules of the game... Then why?... The outbursts follow one another in more rapid succession... Irresistible... Why? Oh, for noth-

19

ing... just anything makes them laugh, that's well known, they need so little... Why trouble to look? Nothing that has anything to do, even remotely, with what just happened. Who does he think they are? They're much too polite, too well-bred to make so bold as to comment and criticize right away like that, as soon as they're by themselves... They are much too worldly-wise. They would be shocked if one of them suddenly took the liberty of committing this incongruity, this gross simplification...

They all know well, without a word having been spoken, that laughing at nothing, really at what is meant by nothing... everything that is most harmless, frivolous, slight... nothing you could say, that you could remember... just that kind of laughter, interrupted by short outbursts, halts... resumed, endlessly prolonged... is between them and him a signal he is bound to receive, similar to messages produced by subtle and complicated chemical reactions, formulated after a long evolution, and which ensure the functioning of a living organism.

Lean toward the other, quietly filling his pipe, push the stone animal to the side of the table, near the bottles and glasses, raise one finger and say: Do you hear them? and together listen... scrutinize... I may be mad. But it seems to me... The other becomes motionless, the other lends an ear... What's that? —Don't you think that laughter... a bit too insistent...

—Yes... those young people seem to be rather excited... It must be fatigue, don't you think? after a long
day... —Probably... his head nods assent, his lips
stretch... —In any case, they are delightful. They
seem to be very close. —Yes, very close... Yes,
aren't they? Delightful... So affectionate...

That's true, it was touching, he felt moved when
they leaned toward him, when they patted his cheek
affectionately, when they withdrew to allow the two
old lunatics, those amiable maniacs, to start their end-
less discussing... Childlike laughter... fresh voices...
pert gestures... velvety scratches, kitten bites, playful
puppies cutting their teeth on dog-eared manuscripts,
old books... teasing little girls who climb on the knees
of old fogeys, run their fingers through the white locks
on their necks, tickle them... and they make no move
... Heads raised they let the cool drops trickle over
them, caress them... How silly people are at their age
... Anything at all makes them laugh. They are light-
hearted.

He should pull himself together, shake himself... It
is time to attend to serious matters. Already the other
has called him to order... he holds out his heavy hand
toward the animal, he pushes it into the middle of the
table, he turns it around, examines it... Imperturbable.
Perfectly quiet and sure of himself. Quite evidently,
he feels in perfect security. With that set there in front
of him, who could do anything to him?... The bubbles
of laughter burst against it, the laughter bounces
against it, the laughter glances off it, the laughter

21

bounds back to them up there... boomerangs... kickbacks... The quiet voice envelops us, the words it is slowly pronouncing protect us on all sides, mount guard... What is there to fear? Who can threaten that?

How do you mean who? But how could you not know that, without making a move, as soon as they are settled, shut in up there, they can dispose of an immense force, they possess enormous power... One single invisible ray emitted by them can turn this heavy stone into a hollow, flabby thing... One look is enough. Not even a look, a silence is enough... You didn't notice a while back? You didn't feel anything when you said: Why, it would deserve to figure in a museum?... You didn't notice a sort of eddy in that silence?... —An eddy? —Yes, when you said that: figure in a museum... —That's true, I did say that. Exactly: in a museum. I'm ready to repeat it. —Oh, I beg of you, say it. Say it again. Repeat it... with that look of conviction... Hold me back... They are pulling me away, they are snatching me from you... Hold me very tight... I am being carried away... Do you hear them? They're calling me, they're bewitching me, they're luring me up there, with them, toward everything that babbles, skips, rolls, sprawls, leaps, nibbles, squanders, bungles, destroys, mocks... toward offhandedness, indifference, flightiness, frivolousness, thoughtlessness... Hold me back, so I won't take this awful old stone animal set there in front of us and throw it with all my might against the wall... Do you too hear that noise upstairs? Come out here, come

22

and see... They open the door, they lean over the bannister... What happened?... They come down... —You see what I did with it? Come and sit down, come here, close up, so we can enjoy ourselves together... let's put on a record by your favorite singer, let's turn on the radio, let's dance...

They're sucking me up... save me, protect me, repeat that again: Deserves to figure in a museum. Yes. Perfectly. In a museum... Quick... take it, wrap it up, carry it away, put it in safekeeping. Well watched-over. Protected. In a glass case. With unbreakable panes. Among others—as well guarded. Put there for all time. May the gaze of countless devotees give it a patina. May the care of generations of curators guarantee its survival. And may they up there, once they've emerged from their lair, be led in awed groups before the eyes of the guards. Be humbled. Who dares to move? May they in silence, cautiously gliding over the waxed floors, stopping at a sign, a brief order, from the guide, listen respectfully to the time-honored observations. What duffer, what insensitive ruffian, over there, back there, is letting himself be diverted? Looking elsewhere? Smiling? Degenerates. Asses. Zeros. Absolutely impervious. Impermeable. Even if you catch them early, when they still seem malleable, educatable, and take them there, force them to look. Imagining that what they have before their eyes gives out something sufficiently percussive to penetrate the most rigid, the most dull-witted, the most immured. Useless to force anything. I remember the shock I once had, when my father...

and yet that didn't happen often... it was such a joy...
I was so grateful to him... But now, look at them, look
at these privileged youngsters, turning up their noses
at art treasures...

But perhaps without meaning to do so he had been a
bit abrupt with them? It sufficed to have patience.
To let things take their course... At times it was
possible to catch on their faces looks that were more
attentive, that lingered... And right away, like a
mother cat that brings young rabbits, birds, to her
young, steps aside, watches them devour and purrs,
licks her chops... he, giving a brief glance to make
sure that the beneficent rays that emanate from these
sculptured stones, from these painted canvases, fall
upon them, that for this they are at the right distance,
in the right spot... Look, take my place, stand where I
am, here, to one side... your back to the light you'll
see better... pushing gently before him, standing just
anywhere, looking at nothing... nothing but them, to
follow what goes on in them... at times being unable
to prevent himself, knowing how dangerous it is, from
helping, speeding a bit... It's lovely, that, eh? isn't
it lovely, eh?... And they curl up like snails, like
porcupines, draw in their horns, stiffen all their quills,
they are mere shells, balls around which he moves...
It's his fault, he knows it, he was clumsy, he made a
movement that was too bold, too heavy... they are so
sensitive, so delicate... they can't bear this touching

... the greatest precautions must be taken... The tender, viscous, soft flesh quiveringly retracted, they shut themselves in... impossible to reach them... Now to get them to come out of there... they can remain like that for days, for months, perhaps forever...

He walks around them... his voice is cajoling... underneath his gay exterior it's impossible for them not to perceive his distress, his entreaties... Very gently he tries to bait them... he offers them from a distance ... without insisting: How funny... that's amusing... Look... But above all he should not have used this word, the imperative of this verb, his tongue slipped, he doesn't want to insist on anything... Come, come, here everybody is free... he's talking to himself: Very amusing that one there, with his ruff... He was the favorite... he seems to perceive in the balls bristling with quills, in the smooth, closed shells, a sort of movement... Something filters through to the outside... like a trail... He was the king's best friend... But later... Something is undoubtedly oozing from them, a bit of salivary substance is running... But later... Moreover it's not to be wondered at, this man has a wicked look in his eye... His mouth... there is a crafty expression in the pucker of his lips, he looks deceitful, don't you think? They come with precaution, they move slowly toward the choice food that he is holding out to them, they feel it, swallow it down... And he is satisfied. When you've had such a close call, you give up your former demands, you gratefully accept a lesser evil.

Motionless beside him, agglutinated to what he is

showing them, they become saturated, they are swelling, and he rocks them, he wraps them up to keep them nice and warm, he looks at them smiling, dozing... listening to swords rattling in narrow, dark alleyways, in vaulted chateau halls, in palace doorways, watching the swirl of silk capes, eyes shining under velvet caps, through the slits of black masks, blood spurting from torn doublets... Gently, with light tickles, he risks reviving them, he makes them open their eyes... This picture was painted when he was still the great favorite. It was painted as a present for the king...

They turned toward him... They've forgiven him, haven't they? They have confidence in him? Without their retracting he can... they will let him... They owe him this reward... this well-deserved little tip... they will allow him as though in passing... what is called without touching it... it has so little importance, is of no consequence, it's mere politeness... before they turn away they will allow him to say as though he were talking to himself: all the same, it's not a bad job, that little number. All the same, that's damned fine... A pure formality, a brief genuflexion, a gesture of the hand that dips into the holy water and makes a rapid sign of the cross... out of habit, out of fidelity to tradition. Even nonbelievers do it when they've been accustomed to do it since childhood... He watches them for the slightest sign of acquiescence... don't the rules of propriety demand it in such cases?

But they appear to hear nothing, they turn away, they frisk about excitedly, riotously, they push one another, punch and dig their elbows into one another, they are laughing... Oh, look at that one, do, I beg of you, look at the face on that one...

This, and yet he had known it in advance, was what his naïve wiles, his cowardly concessions were inevitably bound to lead to... He is being dragged through the galleries by them, from time to time flopping onto a bench, staring before him at just anything, without seeing it... Everything around him grows dull, everything contracts, closes, hardens...

Nothing vibrates, radiates, emanates, flows, overruns... There is nothing... nothing worthwhile... A rough stone, dirty gray, crudely carved. A dumpy, lumpish, rather shapeless animal... No, it's nothing, I don't know what it is, no it was not me, it was at my father's, in his cellar... But do look at that one, look if he's not a beauty, if he's not a rascal... Ah, you scamp, you're a nice brute, good old dog... Ah, want to bite eh, want to play...

They are observing without missing a thing, his shrugging shoulders, his embarrassed, immediately averted eyes, his blushes, his falsely vivacious tone, the pats of his trembling hand... all these awkward, pitiable efforts, to stand apart from, to disavow the unconscious creature who quietly rises, walks toward the mantelpiece, holds out his arms...

How one would like, wouldn't one? to warn him, alert him. How one would like, but one doesn't dare, to let this noble friend, who came in all innocence to pay a visit, know into what den, what trap, he has fallen... we are caught, surrounded... enemy ears are listening, enemy eyes are spying upon us... beware, everything we do, everything we say now can be held against us, involve heavy penalties... there he is approaching, taking in his hands... aware of nothing, miles, hundreds of miles, from suspecting...

But of course, how could he? How could he be distrustful of anything whatsoever, this coddled child, this comrade of our former light-hearted games, this stranger from out there where another order, other laws, reign... where they classify as morons, where they relegate among the pariahs, where they outlaw people who have the scandalous impertinence to take up their stand before an object of the cult, a sacred object that everybody piously reveres, put their hands on their hips, throw their heads back and burst out laughing: Oh, do look at that, that "beauty"!... Look at the face on her...

How could he understand, imagine? even if they explained it to him, he wouldn't take in anything, he wouldn't believe you, he who grew up, who had always lived, without ever leaving it, even for a few seconds, in the peaceful, harmonious world in which quite naturally, quite spontaneously, being sure of everybody's approval, anybody can rise and walk with their hands outstretched, with eyes dilated, shining, approach, then back off to see better... What is it, tell me, this sculpture? It looks interesting... contemplate it a long time, and turning off-handedly to those present say proudly, out loud: It's very fine, that, don't you think so?

There's nothing to be done about it, all you can do is to submit... Impossible to try to put him on his guard. That would be breaking with our secret, our tacit conventions, transgressing the never-formulated interdictions, known to us alone, which no one on the outside should suspect. All those who come here must be persuaded that among us too everyone is free... Come now, don't try to get out of it, what's the use? you'll have to go through with it. Approach it the way we do... you have no choice...

But I don't want to... I don't see anything... It's true, I feel nothing, there is nothing... Don't push me, it's a provocation. I'm only doing it, you know that, because I am forced, coerced by you, my voice, you hear it, is colorless, gone faint, my lips are hard to open when I repeat after you, since you demand it: Yes, it's very fine... And you see, I turn away immediately, I go up to you, my fingers clasp your shoulders, caress your hair... And you, yourselves, tell me, what did you do today. Your fishing trip? What did you bring back?—Oh, nothing much... They stretch themselves a little, they stifle a yawn... The day has been a long one, they had gotten up early... I believe that it's time... They rise... and inside him something breaks off and falls...

While they climb the stairs, already laughing among themselves, then pitilessly close the door, his voice which, as though detached from him, has followed them, which is up there with them, his hollow voice, gone limp, like a cast-off garment collapses... He is like an actor who continues to play his role in a hall

29

which the audience has left, like a lecturer who strives to speak as though nothing were wrong, before empty seats.

The thing that until the last moment had remained attached somewhere in a hidden recess has been roughly pulled off... something in him which had risen up, had stirred, when they approached, when they pushed him in front of them for him to come and look with them... And suppose a miracle had taken place... suppose they really had been attracted... drawn on by an air current... suppose a puff from out-of-doors had swept in through a gap that the outsider had opened by rising and advancing in such an impetuous rush... suppose by obeying with such alacrity his imperious nod, by hastening to make room, to push aside the bottles and glasses, they had seen in him what he was: the respected representative of a universally recognized great power, supported by the adherence of thousands, of millions of people... among the best... They are the salt of the earth. They are the strongest. They are invincible. Invulnerable. They ignore, they do not allow the obtuse laughter of dumb brutes, of sluggards, to reach them...

Loafers? Really? You think so?... It is your opinion, as head-teacher, that there is no hope?...

Silence that endures, is unending... These are evidently questions to which one does not hasten to reply. It is a serious matter to confine in rigid categories, to pin labels on something that is still fluctuating, changing... Of course, there is always hope... But... clearing his throat, tapping as though embarrassed, exasperated, with his closed fountain-pen on the copybooks, the notebooks scattered across his desk, leaning over to look more closely at them... —Yes, it must be said, there is here a lack of curiosity... a sort of atrophy... In the hollow that has been dug inside him the words reverberate, are sent back to him... Sort of atrophy... Yes, a lack of flexibility, a sort of rigidity. It's like a muscle that doesn't work. No matter how hard you try... All the teachers agree on this point. Some have seen in it a perverse intention, a need to destroy, to destroy oneself... a sort of determination to resist at all cost... —Ah, yes? To resist? Resist? At all cost...

There it is, he sees it, a faint glow at the end of the dark corridor, a light... he runs toward it... Yes, it's that: resist. That happens, doesn't it? But then that, that comes from me... —From you? I'm surprised... —Yes, from me... in a breathless voice... from me. I have made some mistakes. My desire to share. To give. To forcibly feed. Without considering that for someone so young it is indigestible, it is irksome... I am the guilty one. *Mea culpa, mea culpa, mea maxima culpa.* I have only myself to blame. I am unpardonable. The insensitive brute is myself...

The other observes him with an indulgent, commis-

31

erative expression... He is familiar with that: first consternation, humiliated resignation, rage... Do whatever you want with him, punish him, expel the loafer, the little good-for-nothing, he doesn't deserve what is done for him... that will teach him... he'll go to work with his hands... Then as soon as anyone dares touch him, rushing forward to protect with their bodies their little darling whom a common enemy threatens... It's even moving... —I believe that you exaggerate. You accuse yourself unjustly. There are children, and I know many, who would be only too happy... who would avidly seize upon what you lavish with such generosity... In the case of bright pupils, on the alert, curiosity, the desire to know, are predominant... what you propose to them induces a state of excitement... you know that well... it's this that wins out... —Yes, I see, yes, thank you, yes, I understand...

Rising, taking leave, taking flight, fleeing across the sad playground covered with gravel, with cement, down the hideous corridors smelling of damp dust, of disinfectant, along the dreary glassed-in classrooms where mediocrities docilely swallow bland porridges... The meek, the weak, like he was, he, the most dutiful, the best behaved of all, he, the joy of his teachers, the pride of his parents, he, the good pupil, so brilliant, always on the honor roll, modestly satisfied with his reports filled with good marks, piles of unreadable books brought back from prize-day ceremonies, heavy with their stiff bindings of imitation leather, their thick gilt-edged pages...

32

Fleeing from there, running toward them... Impatient to join them, to find again in them this secret particle of himself that all his life he had helped to crush, that he had thought was buried and which had come to life again in them... hastening to recover that, what there was that was best in him...

They had known how to keep it, to preserve it in themselves, they let it bloom freely in broad daylight, they who have always refused compromises, abdications. They who dare—they have the courage—when the moment comes, if such is their desire, their whim, slightly to stretch themselves, stifle a yawn, rise perfectly naturally, take leave, go...

But why just at this moment? when hardly a second ago they were listening, themselves asking questions... They can be so supercilious... anything will do... they react at times to the slightest provocation, they are so sensitive to certain stimuli... sometimes they make you think of flowers whose petals irresistibly open or close through the action of light or darkness.

The friend had paraded his knowledge a little too much... they can't bear such displays... what they will tolerate is a few words uttered ironically and as though excusing oneself... they have that sort of aristocratic disdain, an indifference which gives them a certain grace, a certain elegance... which he doesn't possess, that's lacking in him, he is still an unpolished upstart... everybody knows that it takes several generations... Wasn't it he they had in mind... when they mentioned—and he had felt himself blushing— certain looks that they couldn't stand... "certain looks flushed with intelligence." Despite his embarrassment, his discomfort, he had admired them. You'll have to admit that's pretty neat... Sometimes, with the ease and grace of lords of the manor, without ever looking, as though in spite of themselves, they come up with delightful inventions...

No, it's not the friend... not only him... he himself had to... but all he did was to follow them, alone he would never have dared approach without being encouraged by them... But he had perhaps let himself go, he hadn't succeeded in controlling himself... perhaps, when he listened to those explanations, and himself asked questions, there was in his manner, in his tone, an excitement that was underbred... perhaps his look had become "flushed"... No, if that had been all, they would have shown forbearance... they would have let it pass...

There had been more... They perceived in his attentive, devout manner something a bit dubious... a slight swelling, puffiness... the effect of their presence... like a blister that forms on the skin because of the heat... Taking advantage of the fact that they had come up to him sweetly—wouldn't simple politeness oblige them to do so—he wanted to make them a demonstration, present them with a perfect model... Look... since I notice that you seem to be proving your good will, look how you should go about it... how you ought to be... Incapable of resisting temptation, of not seizing the occasion to give them a lesson, to start them on the right path... and becoming frightened right away, trying to efface his traces, sprightly tone, innocent looks, pats, caresses, hugs... Ah, you're a nice creature, nice old doggie... And you haven't told me a thing... How did it go, the fishing trip?... But it's too late. What's done is done. Impossible to return to it. That deserves to be punished.

It's a real feat. An astonishing performance. How can anybody laugh that long?... But you remember, at that age, so little is needed, it's enough for one of them to start... Which one? Any one, you, if you want, you are perfect for that kind of thing, you who always take the initiative, who lead the punitive expeditions even without taking part, you who first rose and went upstairs, dragging the others behind you...

They draw back, they cling to one another. What is happening? Where are we? They look with amazement about them: Are we certain we're in the upstairs room, the room we've always met in before we went to wash, to bed?... The last place where people talk, we always called it that... We have lighted the water-heater and while waiting for the water to heat—you have to—we chatter away... we laugh... Any harm in that? the child eyes open wide to let flow from them and cover him streams, cascades of candor... salutary douche... Excuse us, we didn't think that our laughter would disturb you, and yet we were laughing softly, we thought that through the closed door... —No, that's not it... But since you said that you were tired...

There, that's better. They are coming to themselves again, to us, to a light and reassuring world. Where there is some logic. Where people follow some reasoning. Where it is quite natural for a father to think about his children's health... Yes, it's true, you didn't dream that. It's true, we are quite ready to acknowledge it, you can see to what extent we act in good faith, we said a little while ago that we were going to bed... the day had been long... country air is tiring... It's true that we did say that. But afterward, while waiting for the water to heat, we revived, isn't that normal when you don't have to make an effort any longer, when we're just among ourselves? —Yes, that's normal... —So thaa... t's it... Brra-voh!!... —But just tell me... since, as I realize, you are so frank and sincere... tell me just that... in addition to being tired, which was true, that I don't deny... there was... Pitying, grieved looks... —There was what? —There was... But you're going to make fun of me... —Not at all, go ahead, say it... —You're going to think I'm mad... Good-natured laughter... —That may be, a bit mad... But what difference does that make?... All the same, go ahead... —Well, when we spoke of that sculpture... And when you... when I... They stroke his hair, his cheeks... —That's true, you are mad... It's true, you're fit to be tied, darling... Oh, watch out, I'm going to start laughing again, watch out, hold me back, what will he not think? What is it going to mean this time?... —Why nothing, nothing, as you see, I'm laughing too, I'm laughing till I cry... the way we do when we've just escaped some danger, when we've had a close call, so close, if you knew, and find ourselves here among familiar beloved objects, lying between smooth sheets, being cared for by gentle hands...

If you knew what I saw... where I was... —Come, come, later... not now... Rest, don't think about it any more, forget it... —Yes. I just want to tell you... was it a nightmare? It's not true, is it? —No no, it's not true. Why no, of course, it was the fever, it was delirium... What an idea! You've never moved from here, you did not leave this nice quiet room... the sweet-peas, the flowered percales... the polished oak door that gently closed on the upper room where the young people retired after a long day, after having so graciously taken leave...

They look so frank, so affectionate... They must get along so well... It's really fortunate... Seeing you, the hardened old bachelor that I am sometimes has regrets... If we could be sure in advance... I have been a coward, I haven't dared take the risks... His gaze settles at a distance. There is on his face an expression of gentle indulgence, of detachment... he knows, he understands the turmoils, the transgressions of those who have remained in the century, who have chosen to accomplish their mission otherwise... we should not judge anyone... they are different, that's all... they have other concerns... but there must be many compensations... He lends an ear, he listens...

It seems to me that it keeps you from feeling your age...
it must be a perpetual renewal... —Yes, a renewal.
Yes. That's true. You're right. Yes. Yes. Yes.
Renewal.

Everything is moving away, wavering, assuming an
unreal look... as at the onset of an epileptic fit, an
attack of St. Vitus's dance... One must control oneself,
show nothing... with all one's strength cling to what
is about one, look about one... this peaceful spot, filled
with cheering objects, this charming old friend who
has come for a neighborly visit... What fair wind...
You're always glad to meet each other, to chat... The
young people are a bit boisterous, a bit tiring, they've
gone up to bed, they've shut their door, we are alone,
contemplating that, that sculpture set there between
us on the low table... A superb piece...
But now it is rising in him, impossible to hold it
back any longer, impossible to contain it, it would
explode in demented gesticulations, in indecent cries...
he must try to dam it, he must lift the valve as gently
as possible, allow a thin trickle to escape, avoid an
attack by inducing a slight blood-letting... Yes, yes,
yes, yes, you're right, yes, I am happy, yes, real joys...
but you know... I know very well that it's stupid...
but I must confess to you... When you attach importance to certain things, as you and I do, then a certain
lack of sensitivity, a certain, yes, a certain contempt...
—The other nods... —I understand you, I believe that
I too would find that disagreeable... But it seems to
me, still, I don't know very much about it... His

expression becomes a bit vague, it is as though there were spreading over his face a fine film of boredom... But I should have thought... Don't you think that it can be cultivated, that it can be inculcated...

It is no longer possible to contain what springs from him and writhes in helpless rage, in suffering... Ha, cultivate, you make me laugh... ha, inculcate... Just try it... Lie down before them, debase, lower yourself, offer your bleeding heart to slake their thirst, they will spit on it, they'll smear everything... Oh forgive me, I don't know what's the matter with me... excuse me, wait for me just a few moments, one second, I'm just going... I must...

He leaps up, goes upstairs, turns the doorknob... Why is the door shut? He is whispering... Let me in... —Yes, right away... Wait a second... We closed it because it kept opening and shutting... You can't stand doors knocking... There... Faces with soft innocent curves, with limpid, wide-open eyes... Why, what's the matter? —It's because it's late... You said yourselves... I thought... you hadn't the strength to stay a minute longer... —Did you want us to stay? You should have said so... —No, I didn't want anything, no, all right, very well, all right, all right, that'll do. He goes back downstairs, all the blood has ebbed from his face, his heart is pounding...

Forgive me. They say that they are tired and then they sit up chattering, tomorrow they'll be white as sheets, they'll be complaining.

In the silence, in the emptiness, now it unfolds, tautens the contours of this back, of this belly, of this muzzle, of this ear like a stone wheel. They are gently vibrating... waves are spreading...

How can idiotic titters... what can they do?... What can we do to it, to your big animal?... Ah you poor crackbrain, you take things so to heart. So complicated. A bit persecuted around the edges, admit it... They climb onto his knees, they tickle his neck, they pull his beard... We didn't intend to be mean... As soon as you showed us that our laughing exasperated you, right away, as you saw, we stopped... we just wanted to tease you a little, we like to tease a little, you know that, and how could we resist with you? You do so lend yourself to it... teasing imps, facetious little devils, tender caresses of their young fingers... pert laughter... You'd be glad, that would give you pleasure... come on, say it, if we were like... you know who we mean... You yourself, you remember, you laughed louder than we did, it was so amusing when you showed us that, when you used to organize magic lantern, Punch-and-Judy shows for us... How we laughed, how we clapped our hands, we were so happy together... All those masks, all those puppets that you made so well: the fat girl with the short fingernails surrounded by rolls of flesh... Yes, like those on the madonnas by Flemish primitives... Why Flemish primitives? Why so far-fetched?... And besides, even so... primitive or not, Flemish or not... they were loathsome to look at... ugly like herself, square and swollen like herself... spongy and flabby... letting herself soak... outbursts of laughter greeted her entrance...

Nobody is as good as he is at imitating her voice, her peremptory tone muted the way we do in church, in museums... Look at her. Do you know what she likes just now? Piero della Francesca, it just so happens, precisely him, not to be like everybody else, ha, ha, just when he is all the rage... And do you know what she did during her three days' leave? She went to London, imagine... And do you know why? They're all excited on their benches, they shout... No, no, tell us, we don't know... Well, evidently not for any reason you can think of... for all the things that have just come to the surface in you, you understand? when you heard that name, London... all that you and I see... Why mention it? It's our common heritage, our indivisible property, it must not be broken up, not spoiled... "No, I went to London to see the exhibition of Japanese art at the Tate Gallery. I spent all my time there. It's excellent. It's marvelous..." They shake their hair which has retained the fresh odor of moss, of the silt of shady streams, they dilate their nostrils filled with the sappy smell of meadows, of lawns, they part their lips still wet with tea, with milk porridge... and they laugh... And those over there, do look at those two, you know them... They look as if they were twins... both of them skinny, stooped, dressed about the same way... who get along so perfectly... the ideal couple... look what they

41

brought back from Leningrad... Guess. You'll never guess... the impressionists from the Hermitage Museum in the Winter Palace... —Is that all? Oh no... that's too much... voices weak with laughing... No that's too much, there you're going too far... —Not at all, I'll swear it... he can hardly speak, he too is shaking with laughter... I told them: But after all, that's not possible... That's what struck you most? In Leningrad? And you had never been there? "No. Never."

Oh come very near, come right close to me, you whom I would have chosen among all others, if I had had my choice... you who are untouched, pure, innocent... colts, lambs, kittens... for one of your charming gestures when you stroke your brows, when you place your hands in front of your mouths to suppress a childish yawn... when you leap, run, chasing each other on the stairs, far from the old rough-stone animal, when your light laughter...

It is perhaps he, sitting there opposite me, heavy, squat, saying peremptorily: It would deserve to figure in a museum... That's it, I've got it. That's what made you laugh. Every word should be remembered. Every word—a pearl. How did he say that? "That would deserve"... the highest honor. Result of the most infallible choice. "To figure"... that word alone... but between us is there any need to comment?... "In a museum"... among the sarcophagi, the mummies, the Parthenon friezes, near the Venus de

Milo... in front of which people... he himself told them that... he himself brought them that, this lovely little present stuffed tenderly in their stockings... in front of which people used to go into a trance, sometimes the shock was so great that they lost consciousness... and now... That would have irritated you if we too, standing in front of her, petrified with respect... you would have pulled at our sleeves...

But don't worry, there's no danger, we know very well before what just now certain people are bowled over... Only that's just it... we are not bowled over, we don't fall into any traps, we are strong, independent... our eyes look elsewhere, turn toward the high windows behind which on the paths between the lawns old ladies are throwing grain to pigeons, children are running... toward what has not been examined on every facet, estimated, classified, preserved, embalmed, exhibited, emitting... But how is it possible that nobody here smells that insipid, sweetish odor?...

Silence. Attention. Eyes straight. Contemplate. How long do we have to remain motionless? When will we be allowed to escape? Haven't we sufficiently respected the proprieties? Didn't we come near and didn't we examine as was meet?... We even laid our hands on and caressed it... No, that no, let's not exaggerate things. What would they have imagined, the two high-priests, the two tyrants? No, we didn't carry obedience that far. We showed just what could be demanded in the way of compunction... And then we fled, we took refuge here, and we're bubbling over, we are rolling on the floor, shouting, laughing... Hand me that a minute, so I can contemplate it... hand me... No, wait, I got it first, no, just let me look... Ah, that's what I adore... but wait a second, don't grab it out of my hands like that...

Their heads leaning together, leafing through the shiny pages, their eyes running freely the length of the modest contours, lines that never make so bold—they would not presume—as to detain them, to hold their attention, to seek admiration, to show off... they want nothing for themselves, always ready to be abandoned, forgotten, satisfied if they succeed in filling their roles of mere signs, of mileposts on a road traversed at a mad gallop, in a noise of breakage, explosions, boom, zoom, boom, badaboom, everything leaping, zooming, flying, crashing, burning... motorcycles dash toward steep cliffs, planes catapult in the sky, we're carried away, breathless, seized with vertigo, seized with giggles, toward catastrophe, toward annihilation, faster, further still, again... we the rash, the brash, the devil-may-care... from our wide-open mouths, between our big teeth like the metal teeth of tip-cart cranes, come enclosed in paper bags like those that children blow into, inflate and make burst, in balloons, like those they set afloat then release and watch disappear into the sky, words of ours, words of yours, mass-produced words, ready-to-wear, words that are already worn to a shred, those of the humble, those of the poor... dull and vulgar... if you knew how vulgar... they burst out laughing... not even words, that would be too

44

nice... braying, bleating of flocks, empty-brained like our own brains, the morons, the outcasts... more outcast and more moronic than you can imagine... how could you? how could you follow us to that point, fall so low behind us... even in your most frightful nightmares you could not see to what depths we are capable of descending...

Alone now, leaning toward each other, the two friends turn in every direction the stone set before them on the low table... the two misers tenderly stroke this precious chest, this casket in which there has been deposited, in which is locked up for safekeeping, preserved for all time, something that calms them, reassures them, ensures them security... Something permanent, immutable... An obstacle set on the path of time, a motionless center around which time, arrested, is revolving, forming circles... They hold on to that, seaweed, swaying grasses clinging to the cliff...

It's strange... yet there is nothing in common... I don't know why this animal makes me think... I don't know if you remember... in the Berlin Museum, in the Egyptian sculpture collection, a woman, to the left, as you enter... Yes, yes, I believe I see... —Well, there exists in the line of the thigh, the right thigh, which is in the foreground... there... starting at the hip... He lifts his heavy body on a sudden impulse, stands in the middle of the room, his fat torso leaning slightly backward, puts out his foot, runs his hand the length of his leg... there... you see... Just that... from here to here... Really exquisite... —Oh, yes I see... —Astonishing, isn't it? I was quite staggered by it. One day I spoke of it to Duvivier... Well, believe it or not, he's even more impressed than I am... He told me that it was what had struck him most in that entire Museum... —Oh, there I think he exaggerates. But it is true, for that, I too, would give... They grow silent, deep in thought...

Upon this relic brought back from distant pilgrimages, from long peregrinations through time and space, upon this carefully isolated fragment, set apart, transported, preserved intact and desposited in their common fund, in a simultaneous movement their eyes converge... Like two loving parents hovering above their child, through it they come together, they become one... Moments of perfect understanding...

How fragile, is well known. Who does not know that the most complete fusions only last a few seconds. It is imprudent to put them to the test too often, or for too long, even between near relations, even between ourselves... Wouldn't another form, another line, brought back from elsewhere, suffice to make the two soulmates immediately separate, drift apart from each other, surrounded by loneliness? Isn't that the lot of us all, our inevitable common fate?

Then why when we, a while ago... when we took the liberty... what liberty?... nothing really, less than nothing... not even the slightest pinprick... why right away all that hue and cry?... Why that look of contemptuous hatred when we stood up, when we came over and bowed politely, to take leave. Why, always on the alert, does he observe us as though he were watching for the appearance in us of signs, of stigmata, of symptoms indicative of a hidden ill... an ill that he alone knows?

But how could the poor children understand? How is it possible to believe—and yet we can see for ourselves—that something so vague, so subtle, lodged in the genes, can be transmitted like a hereditary taint from mother to child?

Could he ever have foreseen that in spite of all his care, all his efforts, this ill would develop inexorably in them and become clearly visible, causing in him the same suffering, the same bewilderment as formerly... he was young, recently married... when, unable to stand it any longer, losing all self-respect, all sense of shame, renouncing all decency, he would arrive, spluttering, only to be immediately snubbed: What do you want now? What's the matter? Never satisfied? Still want the moon? Still splitting hairs? —Yes, splitting hairs, that's true? very fine hairs, isn't that so? Scold me, I ask nothing better...

They raise their eyes to heaven... —Ah, what a mess... When there exist so many who are frustrated, who have misfortunes, real ones, and who would never dare... —Yes, misfortunes. Real ones. Acknowledged. Listed. Classified. Written down on cards. All the misfortunes, all of them, you know them all, don't you? That's exactly what I need. That's why I came to consult you. To see if by chance my own "split hairs" didn't appear somewhere, if they had not been accepted, they too, classified... —I'd be surprised, knowing you... —But perhaps they can be found added to something really important... like a corollary, as it were, an adjuvant?...

Shrugged shoulders, resigned sighs: All right, let's see. You've been married how long? Lifeless voice: Three years very soon... But from that angle, I believe that you're wasting your time. You'll have to look among happy marriages. In the file containing perfect marriages. But I realize there is little chance... My case cannot have been considered... —What case? —Well, it's like this... it's a question of likes and dislikes... —Ah, you have no likes in common?... We have a rather large section on that... You should look under travel, nature, sports, means of locomotion, social relationships, receptions, going out, children, domestic animals, country, city, seashore, mountains... —No, I don't think you'll find anything there... It would more likely be in the line of es...esthetic sensitivity... —You're an artist? —No, not at all. But simply... Well, I like... Well, that means something to me... —Then we'd have to look under artistic tastes. —Oh, that's a word... —Ah, you know, here everybody who comes has to lose certain pretensions. This is a place where all kinds of people come for consultation. For the most part, very simple. On the whole, primitive. Sophisticates, the independent-minded can do without us. They must have their own

48

way. He is crestfallen... —Yes, I know. —Well, let's look at artistic likes and dislikes... Leafing through the cards: Museums? —Yes, perhaps... —Doesn't your wife like museums? When traveling, that can of course offer certain disadvantages. But as a rule... It's not that... —Does she prefer frescoes by Raphaël to the Sistine Chapel ceiling? Is that what is so heart-rending? No, don't laugh, it's more serious... —Oh, "serious," undoubtedly... with an emphatic nod... "tragic" would be more suitable!

At the next table an old white-haired man looks to one side over his glasses, leans forward, whispers: But it's terrible, she doesn't at all like... —What? She doesn't at all like? Not art? At all? You really could have noticed that before. All the more so since among people like yourselves, it is by visits to exhibitions, to museums that, very often, everything starts... —No, it's not that she doesn't like... She has her likes, of course... —But not yours, eh, petty tyrant? And it's for this reason that you suffer, that you have ceased loving, that you are wasting your greatest treasure... that you make us waste our time... It's shameful. What a spoilt child... —No, no, clinging, imploring, don't think that, I would sacrifice... I could bear without reacting... better than others, perhaps... —Yes, people say that... —No, that's true, I assure you... But when I'm in the presence of something from which this thing emanates, spreads inside me, something for which I would give... well, it's enough for her to be there near me, for me to feel, coming from her, a sort of counter-current... nothing more

49

comes through, everything dries up, dies out... And my feeling for her, too... as though she had committed... I know, I am unforgivable, I despise myself, I am a monster... Who can help me?...

They pucker their lips, with a pitying look they lean over, they hunt... —You're right, there is no provision here for your case. Fortunately, in fact. Where would it lead to? Who could respond to such exigency? You must resign yourself. Suppress your bad feelings. Let's see, what could we give him to help him when that takes hold of him?... Everything we have is much too crass, too simple... —But that's what I want. I came to you for that reason. I must have something broad, thick, to crush that, when it begins to stir inside me, to swarm everywhere... something I could lay on it at the right moment, just when I feel it's starting... —We must look under maxims. *Vox Populi*. Wisdom of the nations... Here is all I can find... Show me... You see, we have nothing to give you but: "There's no accounting for tastes"... He seizes it avidly, he bows, he expresses thanks... You must repeat that to yourself, you must get that firmly in your mind, it can perhaps relieve you: "There's no accounting for tastes." I realize that it is not what you needed. But does one ever know? If you repeat it often enough... There are people a bit like you— less contaminated than you, it's true, in better health than you, more resistant—well, the fact is... they are much better off for it.

—Yes, thanks, yes, "There's no accounting for

tastes," yes, one should not make impossible demands, set one's heart on the moon... There's no accounting for tastes... Everyone is free. Everyone is alone. We die alone. That's the common lot. Yes that's it. Thank you very much. Yes. There's no accounting for tastes...

Everyone, you know, is not of our opinion. Not at all of our opinion... The other takes the pipe out of his mouth, holds it in his raised hand... —Who, for instance? —Well, Gautrand... Believe it or not, he examined this animal closely and he thinks... in his opinion it dates from a late epoch, copied from a current model... In short, it did not excite him... —Indeed... the friend puts the stem of his pipe between his teeth, in his motionless, attentive eyes there is surprise... That excited tone all at once, the sudden aggressiveness in the voice, must appear a bit strange to him... What do you care about Gautrand's opinion? He is always so afraid of being wrong, of not being taken for a discriminating connoisseur... Late epoch or not... Copy or not... It seems to me that one has only to look... He stretches out his pudgy hand and lays it peacefully on the animal's back... —Are you sure? You think so? Yet Gautrand has deflated a good many false values... his voice is trembling... He knows more about it than most people... and I too, I must say that at times, I wonder...

The friend quickly withdraws his hand, in his eyes there is mingled surprise and fear... the dismay of someone who thought that he was in the company of a friend and who all at once sees him change face, voice and tone, who suddenly feels on his wrist the sharp cold of handcuffs, hears the catch, can't believe his senses... struggles... —But I don't understand... You yourself a little while ago... you said to me... He hears a slight snicker... —But I, who am I? What proofs have I given? Have I ever, myself, like Gautrand, discovered anything whatsoever? Do I own any collections? I, too, see here... now when I turn it to this side, I think it has a funny look... facile, isn't it? ha, ha, a bit vulgar?... Don't look at me like that. I myself am not certain that I possess absolute taste... I may be wrong, eh? Why not? I'm quite willing to acknowledge it. I am quite **willing to** submit... Don't look so scandalized. I'm modest, I am quite willing to renounce my former errors. I yield to the authorities when they are on the right side. I wonder how I could have...

I must have been mad to separate myself from my nearest and dearest, to break such close ties and adore this poor thing, to go into ecstasies before this junk... But it's finished. No more heart-rendings. No more separations. I am one of you, oh you up there. You, my next of kin, you, my own people... They come running... they take me in their arms... Yes, you can see, we are with you, we'll not separate again, everything is smoothed over... No, don't squeeze me like that... No, let me go, I don't want to, I'm afraid...

no, leave it alone, don't take it from me, I'm attached to this animal all the same, I am, you understand... If I abandon it... Don't touch it, it's sacred. To defend it I would... For it...

They gently unclench his fingers, they lift it and turn it around in the light... a poor thing... Their strong yet gentle hands hold him back... He is stammering... A poor thing... Yes, it's true... You knew it? —Well of course we knew it. It knocks your eyes out, come, come. Forget it, let's leave this room, look at us. Their fresh happy faces surround him, their fresh laughter sprays over him... How charming they are... They do not need to study either the early or the late epochs, they only have to give one glance...

Their mobile, agile, light minds leap, let themselves be carried along, tossed about, swept along by all that moves, unfurls, comes apart, glides, swirls, disappears, returns... hardly perceptible slow apparitions... sudden loomings, unforeseen shocks, repetitions with infinite shadings... reflections... iridescences... Nothing revolts them so much as to become motionless, to settle down, to let themselves fill up and doze off with the blissful smiles of overfed babies... everything you desire, everything to which you aspire, poor old madman... But stop thinking about it, give up, come, throw yourself into things body and soul the way we do...

He utters little senile cries of excitement, of satisfaction, he opens wide his toothless mouth, he wears a beatific smile... Yes, I am following you, yes, there now, here I am, I'm going to surprise you, I am

53

younger, stronger and have more dash than you think... you'll see, you won't need to exclude me any longer, to abandon me... I'm one of you, with you...

With us, really? With us, then, all of a sudden. That was quickly said. And we accept him, we don't put him through any tests? We say no more about his past, which is pretty deep-dyed nevertheless, no questions will be asked, nobody will deem it advisable to ask him how it happens that a single word of disapproval uttered by a certain Mr. Gautrand should be enough to cause the collapse of all his great enthusiasm? It would have sufficed, I can promise you, for this Gautrand to tell him that the shape of the ear, there, this fold, guarantees that this animal is an absolutely authentic product... such as can only be seen in the museums... of Mexico City, of Lima... for him to dismiss us contemptuously as lazy, ignorant creatures... You saw his expression, when we approached respectfully, when we were about to touch... his movement, yes, of near repulsion... what, our impure hands could dare? How could we, how could we have the audacity to pass judgment? But that's just it, Gautrand has spoken. He came and left his stamp. The object can be thrown out. And he, set free, light of heart, can move over to our side. But it's not that easy, my friend.

He hears their tittering, their whispering... they're consulting together, they have sniffed the fake rallying... You know perfectly that he is one... Yes, he's

54

on their side, he is one of them, on the bottom rung of the ladder... He would like to climb up, sit on the topmost rungs, there where are to be found, yes... slight outburst... the top-notchers... —With the smug pedants?... —No, keep quiet, will you... What are you thinking of? How do you dare? They are erudites... They're a caste, they're a sect, they're a secret society... their words hiss, lacerate him... You always see them together, like seeks like... There is between them, you noticed it, a family resemblance. Yes, all of them have the same heavy, dull contentment... The mutual esteem of the well-provided-for. And the same idea of "work"... they burst out laughing... of "effort," their work, the effort they exert, day after day... never shirking... never disheartened, weary... Ostrich stomachs. Gluttony. Avidity. Gleaning everywhere, amassing, hoarding, to be sure never to be caught short, never to "want"... You know his anxious look of an old lunatic when all at once in his presence one of them exhibits something that has escaped him, that he has not seized upon... That embarrassed, demeaned expression, that colorless voice... No, I don't know... No... Where did you see it?... And the satisfied fat cat making people admire his treasures: Imagine, I found it one day long ago in a little book that had gone unnoticed, written well before so much appeared on Etruscan art... Or else, perfidiously playing the role of modesty: Oh no, I really deserve no credit... That was all people talked about some ten years ago...

And coiled up in a corner, in each one, an unsated, throbbing desire... to possess still... just that... a thing that is not acquired, that is given you... that an unjust fate has distributed without rhyme or reason to the least deserving, to the malingerers, to the loafers, the drab, the spoilt, those who wear themselves in a sling, incapable of carrying out any irksome tasks, of accepting any discipline, their sick memories rejecting what is wholesome... searching through garbage cans, feeding on refuse, on pieces of rubbish... on rottenness, which for nothing on earth... it nauseates you... but they batten on it, that fattens them up, they thrive on it, these "creators," these "artists" do... Semi-cultivated? They? You're too generous. More like one quarter, one eighth... There's one of them, over there, look at him strutting about, surrounded by ignoramuses like himself. But just wait a minute, my young friends, let's have a look... let's examine that... I thought as much... Is it possible? But that's cynicism... Cynicism! Not on your life, that would be too perfect, you give him too much credit. The poor thing sincerely believes that he was the first to have made this astonishing discovery. And he had no trouble convincing them... Measures should be taken... No, drop it. What's the use? For one who is shown up, ten more suddenly appear.

—Oh, perfect, I can just hear them... You, when you start, you are priceless... —You're too kind... modestly casting his eyes downward, bowing... But I really deserve no credit. We all know the tune...

And turning toward him who is humbly waiting, heaving a sigh... No, undoubtedly there is nothing to be done, my poor friend. No, really, you are not one of us. What curious naïveté makes you hope to come over here, to be a member of our little clan... And you'd be under whose wing? It's enough to die laughing... It's quite unbelievable... Under the authority of Gautrand... Yes, he himself, no less than that, as sponsor...

—But Gautrand, that was to rid myself, that was to escape from, to drive from me that pious devotee, to show him that his opinion, that the opinion... of both of us... that perhaps we are mistaken, that in such matters nothing is hard and fast... no accounting for tastes... it was to prove to him that you were not alone, that others, like Gautrand, agreed with you... —Ah, others like Gautrand... And do you think that we would let ourselves be caught?... "Others" is all very well, "others" is excellent... others like us, right? But to hear you, Gautrand is one of us. Like us. Our equal.

You must really think we are stupid... Here we have Gautrand the supervisor, Gautrand the prof, the board of education inspector, descended in our midst, seated in short pants at one of our school desks...

And suppose against Gautrand, against everybody like him... Yes, go ahead, that's a good question... Yes, answer that: Suppose against all the Gautrands in the world, we had taken the liberty... No accounting for tastes, isn't it so? If we had dared... Horrors. Mortal sin. Heresy. Excommunication. How shameful. What a misfortune. And that it should happen

57

to him. It's unbelievable. It's inexplicable. After trying so hard to protect them, to keep them from bad influences, sullying contacts...

But evil is everywhere, it springs up anywhere, at any moment, when one least expects it, when one believes one is most secure... Right beside us, those little laughs, those sneers... their expressions as they turned to look when he said softly... he couldn't help it... little idiots.

They eyed him for a second from head to foot and then turned away, stalwarts standing firmly on their two widespread feet, chests out, their brawny arms around the girls' shoulders, hands clasping their necks... and the girls leaning against them, laughing... while they point... I ask you, do look at that... There... that face... —That woman's face? —You call that a woman!... That's how I'd like you to be, my beauty... your nose sticking out here... and your eye... oh, that eye... But you know that's a portrait of his lady-love... You know it seems that, thanks to that, she will go down in history... Between you and me, she deserves it, she's really unique of her kind. —Fortunately; you said it, because as for me, if I were with any such beauty... What a guy!... hats off!... —Oh, but how about that, what's that?... A saucepan? —No, a windmill. —An aeroplane... It is not. Look at the title. It's... it's... Oh, really, what do they think we are?

Come, let's leave, it really is unbearable. Toughs.

Future murderers. If he could round up the visitors, alert the guards... police-car sirens should give their sinister wails, the enforcers of law and order should enter, blackjacks at the ready... Where are they? Show them... And he, trembling with impatience, bowed with zeal, guiding the gendarmes, walking backward in front of them, dashing ahead, spurring them on... Here, here, this way... they're over there... I saw them. A little group... I heard every word, their sneers... They were egging one another on... Here, here they are. Look at them, they're the ones... Look at them in front of that... in front of those masterpieces... Quick. Handcuffs. Black Marias. Third degrees. With them there's no other argument. Jeering is forbidden, do you hear? If not, there, take that, and this, that will hold you for a while... But what's the use? At best the brute will pretend to submit. And deep inside, as soon as its wounds are dressed, as soon as its fear is over, that's going to re-form, it's going to well up... What can anybody do? How to stop it? Even from the depths of prison cells, of secret dungeons, it will rise up from them, it will seep through, stinking, withering... they must be destroyed, crushed...

—Hey, listen, did you see those murderous looks? They laugh, lift their elbows... Oh, I'm afraid... We profaned the holy of holies... Laid violent hands... And we haven't the right to touch it, it's sacred... You know there are art-lovers, "connoisseurs"... You know what that's worth, that saucepan there... no, not the saucepan... that gadget over there... —Tell us, how much? Oh darling, I want it, do buy it for me...

59

—It is really unbearable. Go indulge your subtle witticisms elsewhere. —Oh excuse us. But we're not talking loudly. We've no more right to exchange opinions? You, yourself, do not scruple to explain to these little darlings—poor things—it's enough to disgust them for life... —Let's go, come, what's the use in discussing with... with...

But in the look that they cast behind them while he dragged them away, there was a sort of perverse curiosity, a sly nostalgia, a complicity...

In predisposed organisms, on propitious terrains, the slightest germ will develop, proliferate... However much you asepticize, filter, take out of their hands, burn everything that risks contaminating them... fashion magazines, comic strips... turn off the radio, the television, tear down sign-boards, posters... As soon as he is with them his eye becomes a perfected instrument for detecting, perceives everywhere and follows up in them as though on an X-ray photograph, the course of the malady, the progress of the lesions... He will readily spare no effort, avail himself of all his knowledge to preserve them, restore them to health... triturate them, model them... apply the most recently recommended methods to them... depositing in them without their knowledge, leaving within their reach...

Have they come near? Are they busy sniffing, feeding?... Incapable of waiting any longer, he half opens the door, sticks his head in... They don't hear him... stretched out on the bed, they are turning pages, they pause, absorbed... they let him approach, take from their hands, tear up, trample... There that's what I do with them... But where did you get them? And how can you waste your time like that?... He stamps his foot, he shouts, they must perceive in his voice the puerile fury of the weak, childish despair... Well, it's very simple. Do you hear me: I want none of that in my house. And that's that. Period. When all is said and done, this is my house, you're under my roof. You know that I forbid. I prohibit... With dilated pupils their vacant eyes glance off him without seeing him as he leaves...

But they lose nothing by waiting, they'll see, they'll learn that he's the stronger. One day they'll be starved and whether they like it or not, they'll have to eat what they're given, the food that's left in the little captive animal's cage... they'll have to make up their minds... But great attention must be paid, he must take precautions, above all so they won't be able to suspect that he is there crouching, watching... they would turn aside right away.

That's what they got on their set which they had been adjusting for many years, and which records every vibration, however weak, that comes from him, that's what they perceived when he left the table with a gesture that was a bit too brusque, turned away too ostensibly, leaned over, caressed their dog a bit too eagerly... that fear of frightening them and that quivering hope... They know—no trick can mislead them—that he is always turned toward them, inca-

61

pable of leaving, of forgetting them a single second... they felt clinging to them the threads they make him secrete, that slaver with which he tries to envelop them, the slender lasso that he throws at them from behind... and they stiffened, they withdrew violently, they went upstairs, dragging him behind them, giving him hard knocks, his head bumping against the steps...

Their spontaneous laughter, fresh from the spring... Perfectly natural. The rather suspect slight tremolo was a wrong movement, a fault of adjustment, immediately corrected. Perfect naturalness is absolutely obligatory. Each of them knows this without a single word having been spoken, a single sign given... not a trace of the slightest collusion. What collusion, good Lord? Why? Aren't we among ourselves here, at home? In our element. The one that suits us. Yes. Us. Just as we are. Just as God made us. Unchangeable we. We who will have to be accepted. We inside it like fish in the sea, we who nowhere breathe more easily, we who like nothing so well as to frolic about in that... Oh, hand it here... Don't grab like that, you'll tear it... Personally, whatever you say, I think it has immense chic... That's piling it on... Oh look... and the laughter that is always on the point of breaking out spreads irresistibly, comes through the closed door, sprinkles him...

But that's not possible. We disturbed you? Yet we were laughing softly... Not a flicker in their candid eyes, on their smooth faces not a tremor... It's he, he alone who deposited in them... He finds in them what he brings to them. Even if he explained to them, they wouldn't understand... These are such subtleties, aren't they? Tell that to just anybody. Take just anybody as witness. Ask your friend, then... Speak to him about it, just try and complain...

Listen... that laughter... Just listen to them. —What is it? What's the matter with you? —That laughter... do you hear them? Those little titters... sharp as needles... But wake up, don't look so vacant... Those titters like the drops of water that are made to drip on the heads of torture victims... they drip on us, to make us suffer, to destroy us... Don't you really hear them? What are you made of, anyway? No, of course, you can't believe me. You can't believe such deceit as that... The other sits up, staring wide-eyed at him... But how could you not notice when... at the moment when you had the imprudence... when you were mad enough... —I? Mad? Ah, that's a good one... —Yes, mad... leaning over, seizing the animal with both hands, brandishing it in his face... Yes, I'll say so, mad. Fit to be tied... to dare, in front of them, to go and take it, set it there, contemplate it... they rose, they pushed it away, they went upstairs, and now they're defiling, destroying... everything... everything that makes life worth living... look how they make me talk... what grandiloquence, what

63

lack of reserve... see what they're doing to me... they're slowly finishing me off...

In response to his howls of pain, of rage, the door at the top of the stairs opens halfway, prudently they stick out their heads... What's happening? —I really don't know, your father is exasperated. Your laughing disturbs him. He is... quite... I don't know what's the matter with him. I don't understand a thing about it. They come down a few steps, they lean over the bannister rail with a worried expression... —What on earth is the matter? What's wrong?

The friend feeling that he is no longer alone, reassured that the alerted family is supporting him, tries gently to reason with the madman: You see you frighten them. Look how upset they are. They were having fun... —Yes that's so, we were enjoying ourselves, we didn't suppose that that could annoy you... —Personally it did not annoy me. It's your father who imagined that... —That what? What did he go and invent this time? What have we done now? Say it... —Yes, say it to them once and for all. Because I myself would be quite at a loss... I didn't understand a thing, not a single thing.

He says nothing. He hangs his head like a little boy who has just made a scene... No, it's not important... his voice is slightly raucous... Let's forget that I said anything. I didn't say anything. —You see, there are moments... he himself doesn't know why it comes over him. Whatever we do, we have a talent for setting him beside himself. You never know what he wants. You never know what you should do for him to be satisfied... for him to like us a bit... their faces are puckering, their drooping lips are pouting the way children's do when they are about to burst into tears.

They come down the steps one after the other, they fall into line at the foot of the stairs, their skinny arms dangling against their lean bodies, facing the social worker who has finally been alerted by indignant neighbors, and who is watching them, seated erect on her chair, pad and pencil in hand... So say it, stop being afraid. They remain silent, they cast grim looks at their torturer. They nudge one another... The biggest and boldest, finally draws himself up, pushes a lock from off his forehead, clears his voice... Well, it's like this... in reality it's because... One girl suddenly collapses onto the floor, her hair covers her face, she begins to sob... Yes... it's because... we have the feeling... —Yes, I've felt it ever since I was a little child, there is about us... I don't know what... No matter what we do... there's something about us that he detests... Yes, yes... they all nod, they whisper... Yes, that he hates... yes, with deep-rooted hatred... he would like to destroy us... he's ready to kill us... The slightest display... The other day, when I said...

The social worker waves her pencil... —Come, come, if you mumble, if you all speak at once, how do you expect me to understand... It's not very easy at best. What is it, then? Try to explain. What does he hate?... With a slightly vacant expression, sniffling,

65

nodding their village-idiot heads... —Why that's just it... nobody knows. He never says it. But it's enough for us to open our mouths... He won't allow us to breathe... You see, not even laugh a bit... even when he's not present... We were upstairs, the door was closed...

She turns toward him, sunk into his armchair, his head resting on his chest... —You don't allow them to laugh, even among themselves? He rises, he turns toward them entreating eyes... —You know perfectly well that's not true... it's not that... you know perfectly well... One of the girls raises her tear-swollen face... —What do we know? she snivels... It's always the same, no matter what we do... Well, say it, what have I done? He'll never admit it, Miss, he'll never tell you that it's because of that... —How do you mean that? —Why, that... her voice, her intonations are those of a little child... Well that, there, that awful animal... I didn't show it enough respect... I caressed it nevertheless... didn't I? That's not true? —It's true, we all went up to it, we looked at it... but probably not long enough. He holds a stopwatch on all our gestures. If one of us had hung back, he would have thought that we were play-acting. Whatever you do, you're in the wrong. —As for me... she breaks into tears again... when I said... that it was a piece of sculpture from Crete... —No, you didn't say that, you said that it reminded you of Cretan sculpture. —Yes, that's true... sometimes I lose my head, I say anything just to say something... Then he jumped on me, he began to bark... Of what?... assuming a hor-

rible accent... hatred twisting his mouth... Of what?...
he bit me... Then we split, we thought it was
wiser... That's true, isn't it, what I just said? They
nod approval... —That's true, he bit her, we don't
know why... Then we took leave very politely...
Didn't we? You witnessed that?... and we went upstairs. And up there, by ourselves, needless to say,
we wanted to console ourselves, forget about it... She
dries her eyes, she smiles... —Yes, they showed me
some pictures, we laughed... and that's the result...

He listens without speaking, his head bowed... Of
what?... Yes, of what? when all at once, to his
amazement, she made so bold, without authorization,
without ever having deigned to make the slightest effort
to have the right to proceed there where the most
practiced persons, trained at the cost of what suffering,
what sacrifices, what abnegation, venture to go only
with precaution, with fear... she dared to enter with
such offhandedness... she seized upon that as though
it had always belonged to her, she laid her hand on
it with a protective look... he restrained himself not
to push her away brutally, not to give her a rap on the
knuckles... With the assurance of a neophyte, with the
arrogance of an upstart she had... solely to brave him,
certain that in the presence of an outsider he would
not dare take her to task, that his amazement would
keep him from making any move... she had the insolence, relishing in advance his powerless rage, his
suppressed fury... imitating the tone of the old connoisseurs, she dared to say: That reminds one rather
of Cretan sculpture. Then he jumped on her; of what?

and she discreetly drew aside... you must never show an angry cur that you are afraid of its barking... and then calmly, turning away from him, speaking as an equal to his friend, she repeated, while the others, closing in around her, admired her self-possession... Yes, don't you think that that reminds one rather of Cretan sculpture?... and triumphant, leaning toward him, patting his cheek, graciously holding out her hand to the guest, followed by the others who were already stifling their laughter, she withdrew...

The representative of the Society for the Prevention of Cruelty to Children gives him a severe look... Well, I hope you're satisfied, you have achieved fine results. This is your work, these poor frightened, debased creatures, their gaze always turned on you, watching every bat of your eye, weaned of confidence, of love, fearing every moment to displease you, hastening to obey your haziest orders... Cretan sculpture... that was not what you wanted. Cretan sculpture was not said the way you wanted it. The intonation did not suit you. The question, the doubt were not well dosed... not only the doubt: anxious expectancy of your approval was not added in the proportions required. So right away you brought them to this, look at them, lying prostrate at your feet, looking at you entreatingly through their tears... —Cretan sculpture... Wasn't it you who, one day, spoke to us about it? Did I do wrong to remember it? To want to please you? To try to prove to you that you hadn't wasted your time? But quite evidently this is only a pretext, the first one at hand... he can use everything... everything can be used to keep alive his distrust, his hostility... the hatred he has for us...

The investigator unscrews her fountain-pen, opens her pad... So then, let's get on with it, let's summarize. Is it correct that you bit this poor child? Those are, to say the least, strange methods of education.

He straightens up, he shakes himself. Where are we? What is going on? But Miss, you rang the wrong bell, in the wrong neighborhood. Just look around you. See this peaceful room, this old friend seated opposite me, these percale curtains, these sweet-peas, these nasturtiums, these morning-glories which my daughter, yes, this very one, picked from our garden and arranged with such taste in the old vases, this piece of sculpture set on the table between us, a unique specimen which we were admiring... Look at these children... there exist none more cherished... Where is there a trace of a scratch? Who spoke of what bite? —But you know perfectly, sir, that they said that you had bitten them... —Bitten! Show me your legs then, your thighs, your arms... Bitten!... She turns toward them... —Yes, show me. —No, Miss, there's no use, they are bites that don't show... —You see yourself, Miss, they should be ashamed... ah, if I at their age... but they are spoilt, so lazy. Despite the fact that I have them tutored by the best professors, see how they misuse the language... those vulgar metaphors, that tasteless exaggeration...

They jostle one another in front of him, they are speaking all at once... You know perfectly... Oh, what hypocrisy, what low comedy... You know what

69

you did... —What I did? You are my witness, my friend, you were present, what did I do? —Why, nothing, I saw nothing... They throw themselves at the friend's feet, they implore him... Tell the truth. Protect us. What are you afraid of? It isn't possible for you not to have noticed anything... You saw when he leapt up, when he shouted... —Ah that, no, he did not stir from here. He did not utter the slightest cry. —You didn't hear "of what?" yes, "of what?" So fiercely. "Of what?" So full of hate. "Of what?"... Poor child... They took her upstairs, they dressed her wound, calmed her with drops of valeriane, with extract of orange-blossoms... Of what? Of what? Of what? because she... oh, it's too awful... just because she dared to speak of Cretan sculpture... The friend appears to be pondering, trying to remember... —Yes, that's true, your father did say: "Of what?" He appeared surprised. I confess that I too... to speak of Cretan sculpture in connection with this piece... I believe, my little friend, that you were mistaken...

The social worker looks at her watch. —Ah, Miss, you're right, we are making you waste your time. The young people of today, as a result of spoiling, kindness, comradeship don't know what to ask for next... My tone didn't please them. When I heard that howler I didn't show sufficient deference. My surprise offended them. They are so accustomed to being handled with gloves. The fact is, Miss, they are conceited little do-nothings. Just to mention "sculpture," and even more so "Cretan," was a real exploit. I should have gone into ecstasies, stroked her hair, rewarded her... instead

of which I made so bold... And right away they run
and complain, I'm accused of harsh treatment, you are
put to inconvenience... She rises, holds out her hand to
him... —Ah, sir, you are not the only one, we see
many surprising things... But believe me, these children are not the ones to blame. You have spoiled them
too much. Later, life will not be so easy on them. It
is a bad thing to cultivate such touchiness, to make
them into a lot of sensitive plants...

As soon as she has left, they wipe their tears,
straighten their hair and their clothes, they lean over
to kiss him, they hold out their hands to the guest...
Excuse us... We're dead tired. Good-night, have a
pleasant evening...

And there they are already enjoying themselves...
People are quickly consoled at that age... Still gulping
a bit, her face still somewhat puckered, still smeared
with half-dried tears, she is smiling already, she is
laughing with them...

He can't bear any longer the confident gaze turned
on him by the one who never in his life... Do you
know what sin is? A criminal action? No, you don't
know... —Yes I do, of course, how do you expect
that during an entire life?... What do you suppose? of
course there are things that I prefer not to think about.
—What, for instance, do tell me... After all, no, you
don't have to tell me, I know. I know your misdeeds...
the exquisite remorse of people who during their entire

protected lives have never had the opportunity to hurt a fly. Always so peaceful, so detached. Pure. So pure. That laughter you hear... also so pure, isn't it? Innocent, transparent... Just as everything is transparent where you are... They're enjoying themselves, that goes with their age. Ah, we were like them. Impossible to stop. Delightful giggling. Our mother scolded us smilingly. Our grandfather looked at us with that indulgent expression of his, over his newspaper, over his glasses... When you've finished that silly game, that crazy game... Let's have a little quiet there, children...

Excuse me just a second... I just want to go and tell them... —Why no, let them play, they don't disturb me. —No, it's not that... I just want... I'll be back... Rising, going quickly upstairs... just to show them... to point out... to erase everything... start everything over again... knocking at their door... I beg of you... I must come in... He hears a certain stir, whispering... They slowly open, they step aside and observe him with a distrustful expression, pressed close to one another... Well, you look as if you were having a good time in here... That's not my case downstairs... It was not sporting of you to have abandoned me... patting their heads, clasping in his arms their bodies which become inert, stiffen... he cajoles them, rocks them, he tickles their cheeks... just one little smile... just one... he blows... there... Did he hurt her? It's not possible. We never really judge our strength, we forget to what extent these darling children, his flesh, his life, are fragile, vulnerable... Just one tiny thing... Just "Of what?" said in a rather curt tone... Rather curt? Come, come, you'll have to admit, rather curt isn't the word, it was almost savage... they are so tender... at his mercy... He the dispenser, he, responsible for their entire lives, he criminal, unpardonable... look to what a state he has reduced them, look at this nauseating litter... fashion reviews, detective stories, comic strips lying about everywhere... such hideousness, vulgarity... poor debased creatures, driven back to their lair as soon as one of them dared approach the source of life... enter the sacred enclosure... use the language of the masters... "Cretan sculpture"... it's unbelievable... He rose up, he jumped at them, he hit out at random: "Of what?"... an uncontrolled movement, an unfortunate reflex, a criminal gesture...

He is prepared to make amends, they should deign to tell him how... at the cost of what retractions, what renouncements, what betrayals... he will shrink from nothing if he may hope to efface, to make them forget, to obtain their forgiveness... He caresses their hair, he presses the lobes of their ears between two fingers, shakes them gently... I see that you're wide awake, your weariness has passed, then come on down, come, it will be so much gayer... you'll make tea, we'll talk... You will explain to us, my sweet, why this animal made you think of Cretan sculpture... You surprised me, you see, it's a comparison that I had not made...

She should come down, she should enter, she should deign to take her seat among us... Admire her beauty, her knowledge... she will cast the deciding vote, won't she?... Cretan sculpture... You would never have dreamed of it, nor would I... But to tell the truth, why not? if you look at it from a certain angle... in fact if you think about it there's nothing so surprising about that... He takes her by the hand... Come, come quickly, he will end by finding everything strange... Come on down, I beg of you... She withdraws her hand, raises it to her mouth, stretches herself... —No, you don't mean it... They made me laugh, that woke me up... But now I must really go to bed... Tomorrow I won't be able to stand.

Mean natures. Yes, that's it... he feels quite weak... a slight giddiness, as when we're about to lose consciousness... The other opposite him rises, thrusts forward his heavy chest, stretches out his bear's paw and slaps him on the shoulder... —But what's the matter with you? You look quite pale. I must have hurt you... —No... he stiffens, straightens up... No, that's nothing... You must be right... They are mean natures. But it's hearing it. Said like that. Formulated. It's funny, I had never yet said it to myself. Never like that. —But see here, you misunderstood me. I said that if it was correct, what you think, what you imagine... that if it was true that this laughter... which to me appears to be innocent... if it really came from a deliberate intention to avenge themselves in such a petty way, with such sly cold-bloodedness, then, quite evidently, such laughter could only emanate from mean natures. And you know, my dear friend, there's nothing you can do about that. There is no use regretting what one has or has not done, torturing oneself, wasting one's strength... —Yes I know perfectly... —But, once more, that's not certain. If you had not suggested it to me yourself, it would never have entered my head...

It's done. He has turned them over. He couldn't hold out. In a cowardly manner, to clear himself, to save himself, laying all the blame on them alone, he went and denounced them. And now it's too late, the proceedings having been instituted, ineluctably the action will take its course. Here all the movements of flux and reflux, all those comings and goings, those hesitation waltzes to which they are accustomed up there among themselves, where nothing can ever have any consequences, carry with it the slightest penalty— are unknown. Here everything is clear. Unalterable.

The law must consider nothing but the facts. Them alone. Give your name, address and date of birth. Raise your right hand and say: I swear to tell the truth, the whole truth and nothing but the truth. Is it correct that the accused had always refused the care that you were generous enough to lavish upon them? Is it true that out of inertia, out of egocentrism, out of shabby pride, they disdained those delights that are justifiably considered the noblest, the purest, which you wanted to share with them? —Yes, it is true. But perhaps it is because I... —Don't try to confuse... to divert... Answer the question. Is it true? —Yes, it is true. —They hold art in contempt. You yourself declared that. —Well, that's what they show... —Precisely. Here it's what people show that counts, do you understand? —Yes, I understand. —You said that they retired to their rooms just when you were admiring a statue. And that afterward, they laughed with a laughter that was repeated and endlessly prolonged, in the intention of flouting you, of making you suffer, knowing that they would surely succeed in doing so, without your being able to make a move. —That's true. At least that is what I thought. —You have good reasons to think it. There were precedents. Numerous ones. Their court record is far from clear. This is not, I see, your first complaint. Let's see... Six years ago, they rose like that and left under some pretext or other, hardly excusing themselves, it was not very polite, while you were reading to them. Do you remember? —Yes. I was reading them some passages by Michelet. —That's right. Shortly afterward—about a year—when you took them to a museum... —It was not to a museum. It was to an exhibition. —That may be, it is not stated precisely in the report. Shall we say to an exhibition. They turned aside from that canvas—which is very fine—by the master of Avignon. —Didn't turn aside. I exaggerated. They stood there in front of it, but without looking at it. They had that unreceptive, self-centered look... And when I said: It's lovely... —You made a declaration in which you used the expression "turned aside." You were wrong. —Yes. To tell the real truth, I should have declared rather that when I remarked: It's lovely... they remained silent. —That, however, was hardly conclusive. It would have to be proved that their silence was hostile. You know the saying: Silence gives consent? —Their silence was hostile. —Was that all there was? Nothing else? No shrugging of shoulders? A slight sneer or even just one of those faint smiles? —I saw nothing of the kind... —And you have no witness? —No, we were alone. —Then there is no proof. Here, as you were told, we only take into account what may be seen. —Then there is no proof? Really? Silence gives consent... Of course, that is impressive. Very impressive. There have of course been so many other silences concerning which I could have sworn... —Still basing yourself on mere impressions? And we can't take into consideration impressions of this kind. There could have been consent in that silence that day, just for a second, without your knowing it. —Yes, just for a second? Just, even among them? Even among them... does one ever know?... even they, forgetting my presence for once, may have felt a fluid, a current, coming from the canvas... passing over me, to one side of me, even they... it's not impossible... they who are such poor conductors, so unreceptive... it may even have passed through them... That single second is enough, isn't it? One second of repentance permits us to redeem all our sins... —Yes, but if you don't mind, let us return to what can be proved. When they rose, when they went up to their rooms, when they began to

laugh in that manner you describe, and which so affected you... let us come back to that. This time, you
were not the only one who heard them. —No, a
friend was there with me, he listened to them and he
said, I am certain of it... —Very well, take a seat,
we'll look into that. Bring in the witness. Do you
swear to tell the whole truth? Nothing but the truth?
Raise your right hand and say: I swear it. —I swear
it. —Did you hear these young people laughing?
—Yes, I heard them. —And after having listened
to them laugh for a certain length of time, you
said of them: they are mean natures... Wait. Don't interrupt. You later stated to your friend that you had
said: they would be mean natures. —That is to say
that I... —Answer just that point: when you uttered
this sentence for the first time, did you say "are" or
"would be"? Are—in the present indicative, or would
be—in the conditional? This, you understand, is an
extremely important point. Are or would be? Remember that...

Among the motionless spectators there is total silence. And he, seated in the back row, fawns, ducks
his head... in a second it is going to burst out, it is
going to crash down upon them, upon him... He hears
the steady voice slowly articulating: I remember quite
well. I said: would be. Joy. Tears of joy. Release.
He wants to go down on his knees, beg for pardon...
would be—so it was true. Would be—so that's what
he said. Not are, oh no, would be... How could he
have been so low as to doubt such honesty, such perfect
good faith... Would be, would be, would be... every-

thing is still possible, everything can yet be saved... He is no longer afraid of anything, whatever is decided, whatever is ordered, he accepts in advance every judgment, even against himself, above all against himself, he deserves, he alone, every sanction... Yes. I said: would be. Indeed, simple politeness demanded it. How could I have done otherwise?... The whole audience sways and murmurs... —If you could have done so, then you would have said: are?... Everything about him is wavering, he feels a buzzing in his ears, he has a mist before his eyes, as though it came from afar he perceives: Yes. I would have said it. —Why? —Because I would have liked to give him a lesson. A good lesson. He had it coming to him. It was shocking to hear him talking against his children, to me who is a mere outsider... at the same time hoping, of course, as always in such cases, that I would decide against him, expecting to be reassured. Well no, I don't like this pretense, one should suffer the consequences of one's actions: if that's how things are, if what you tell me is true, then they are mean natures. Moreover, at the time, apprehension, fear made him hear "they are." And it's too bad that I should have been unable to refrain from denying it... —But that laughter... let's come back to that... that laughter, which so upset the plaintiff, you did pass judgment on it, just the same... —Yes, it got to be exasperating after a while... if you paid attention to it. Which, had I been by myself, I surely would not have done. Personally, I am quite a simple man. I do not split hairs. I dislike complications. Why delve, why hunt? Life is complicated enough as it is. In all probability, I would have been completely hoodwinked, as they say, although in this case this does not seem to be exactly the right expression. And they would have stopped. Or they would have kept on... What does it matter? These young people are what they are. Neither better nor worse than many others. In any case they can't be changed. They can laugh themselves sick if they feel like it. Live and let live...

He feels delightfully weak, as when we wake up, after a high fever has dropped to normal, when we know that we're entering into convalescence... The little old woman seated beside him, who was listening, her neck outstretched, turns on him her gentle faded eyes... their cheeks soften, pucker, their lips stretch into a nice, toothless smile, their heads nod... What a just sentence has been handed down. How wise it is to bow to it...

No more struggling... What's the use?... We have to understand finally that we've had our turn, and that it's up to them to play...

We'll have to submit, let ourselves be taken in hand... Not struggle, kick when they try gently but firmly to mold us, swaddle us, turn us over and over with looks, with gestures of indulgence, of tender pity. And it's even better to precede them, to appear before them more bent over than the weight of the years would demand, pant a bit more... ah these old bones, ah this old heart... Be touchingly coy... Know how to practice this art. Those who refuse to do so, those who try in a cowardly manner to get out of doing it, are pitilessly called to order, after a brief, mocking glance, by the first bicyclist they've allowed to graze them, when they step too soon onto the street, when they walk too close to the edge of the sidewalk...

They feel snug, withdrawn into themselves, curled up in the gentle, rumpled fragility of a balloon that, with a barely perceptible sigh, collapses... Ah, what do you expect, that's how it is, there's nothing to be done about it... We, believe me, are the first to regret it, don't remain standing, be seated, let me offer you, I'll bring it to you... ah, but the fact is that he's still hale and hearty, he'll bury us all... What keeps him going, you see, is that he has succeeded in retaining all of his interests, his enthusiasms... you must let them follow all of their fads, their crazes, it is a good thing for them to stick to their hobbies... above all avoid opposing them... Approach, as they want us to do, lean forward, look respectfully... and then withdraw. Everyone in his place. Everyone at home. What could be more normal? What more wholesome?

Do we ask you to come with us? Do we take the liberty of forcing you to join us in following with eyes so glassy that they could be taken for real ones the movements of the little ball, your entire body shaking from the jumps and starts of the flippers?*... To listen amidst the din to deliciously vulgar tunes being played on jukeboxes? You have surely never heard them.

* *Translator's note*, reference to The Soccer Game, a very noisy table game to be found in every French café.

To read the comics? Haven't we borne with your sneers, your continual provocations, your contempt for sclerotic, insensitive, conventional, ignorant old men?... Have we grabbed from your hands, to shred or burn them, your well-bound deluxe volumes... untouchable... incunabular... sacred? Have we dared so much as smile in the presence of this animal? We even went so far as to say... to please you... we'll be like them one day... we must make an effort, join in their senile games out of pity... didn't she say... and how I admired her... that it recalled Cretan sculpture?...

And then we shut ourselves in. Free at last... Live and let live... since that's what you call it... yes, since for you that's how it's called... those are words you like... that's understandable, why explain it? Live. Living. It lives. The stone animal lives... dead words spoken by dying people. They mean nothing to us. What is it that lives or doesn't live? What? A jukebox? Lives. The Soccer Game? Come on, raise your hands. Lives. There. Bravo. Of course, it lives. Comic strips? Live. Magazine covers? Live. Advertising? Lives. Strip-tease. Lives. Lives. Lives. Raise hands faster. Higher... Why no, what's that you're making them do? Aren't you ashamed? You brute, you... let's leave them, at present they're doing no harm to anybody, we've only to pay no attention to them, forget them...

The laughter increases, very loud, really good hearty laughter, aimed at nothing, not at us, that's evident, laughter that bursts out, rises and dies down, there, on the spot, among them... It's not their fault if a few tiny drops seep through the door... a slight mist... a cool caress... Heads raised they hold out their faces... a simple-minded smile distends their features... Do you hear them?... My father used to say about us: They are so silly... you have only to wiggle your little finger for them to burst out laughing...

Release. Peace. Freedom. Delicious respect for others which is—how right, how true that is—which is nothing else but self-respect. Live and let live... Free... all cords... all moorings cut... alone... pure... through the big empty rooms, across the gleaming old floors... toward that, just that, in the corner over there, near a window... set there, in offering... no, not in offering, that doesn't offer itself, that doesn't solicit anything. Therein lies its strength. Nothing. From anybody. It is sufficient unto itself. It's there. Come from no one knows where. Torn from no one knows what. Calmly repulsing anything that comes to cling to it: all the images, all the words. Rejecting them. No word can alight, remain on that. No word can merge with that, conclude an alliance with that. No familiarities. It's there. Alone. Free. Pure. Demanding nothing. He stops and stands in front of

83

it: a rough stone carved in the form of a strange animal. No exact name. There should be none. The plate giving the origin, the date, is an insult. A profanation.

Now the operation starts. To begin with, time. Like the waters of the Jordan it withdraws on each side to permit passage... No. It doesn't withdraw. It has stopped. It is a motionless instant. Boundless. An instant fixed for all eternity. A single infinite instant, infinitely peaceful, which that fills. What's that? Why, there's nothing more here, no more petty, precise, coy, beautiful, ugly, coaxing, treacherous, tyrannical, sullying, reducing, amplifying, gossipy, degrading words... toward which, losing all dignity, all instinct of preservation, one must strain, which must be solicited, which must be hunted for, tracked down, for which traps must be set, which must be tamed, brought to heel, tortured. No. Not a word here. In that flowing instant, without shores, without even distant horizons, calm, without end, motionless, nothing stirs... quite motionless... serene, so calm... That... What's that? No. No words. That. No more. There, from the stone animal that issues, that spreads... A movement? No. A movement's disturbing. It's frightening. That's there. That has always been there. A radiance? A halo? An aura? The hideous words touch that a second and are immediately rejected. And he who is there... no, not he, he is this infinite... which that fills... no, not "infinite," not "fills," not "that." Even "that," one shouldn't... it's already too much... Nothing. No word.

And then the waters come together again, time resumes its flow, it is over. All that remains in him is a feeling of immense peace.

The words return, they alight, there's nothing left to drive them away. The docile, slightly inert thing lets itself be wrapped. It lets itself be dressed. About it expert cutters are bustling. Clever hands make it turn around. It stands very quiet while the words are pinned on it, it submits to long fittings. It presents itself to the attentive gaze of the ones who are looking from every angle, it displays its charms. Cleverly assembled words conceal and reveal its forms, scintillating words cover it over. Attired and adorned like that, he can hardly recognize it. It stands rather stiffly, as though conscious of its rank. It demands, it receives, respect.

These words with which it is surrounded are like barbed wire, like the current that runs through it... If the ones who are laughing up there were to make so bold as to stretch out their hands to pat it condescendingly, they would feel sinking into their flesh the barbs, running through them, the discharge.

Seated opposite each other, with the stone animal between them, subtly they adorn, protect it... Who among those up there dared to approach it... Who dared pass through the defenses? Have the insolence to take at random from a formless heap, from a pile of detritus, from an enormous trash-dump that they were digging in: Cretan sculpture, and then try to make that fit? Why, nobody. Nothing. Who heard it?

Who remembers it? To recall it is degrading. It is mad to attach to it the slightest importance. Insane, isn't it? Absolutely disproportionate, outside all reality... How life must have spoiled you, how little real trouble you must have had for you to be able to be engrossed with such futile things... You're right. That's finished, I won't do anything more about it. They can laugh all they want. I don't hear it.

Really not? But is that possible? Is it believable? It really does leave you cold?... The dose will have to be increased a bit. Just a little finer, more insinuating, then immediately interrupted, just a bit more biting, gently slipping, subtle stinging, caress of nettles, a pinch of itching powder... Really no sensation? Nothing? Has he quite forgotten our code language, that took so many years to perfect? Has he gone over entirely to the other side, along with that fat old simpleton over whose face a satisfied smile is stupidly spread? Does he feel so cozy and warm down there, with them? Come on, a little louder, let's hold it... brief stridences... then stop and start over again... until he waits, entirely turned in on himself... until he is divided in two, one part of him drawn in this directon, toward us...

But he thinks he can do just anything, as though we weren't there... when the cat's away the mice will play... cynically daring to recount his escapades, disclose his little solitary excursions, brag about them... In the far room, really? Near the window? Divine? No? Yes. A superb piece... Alone. Far from us, his near and dear, betraying us, hiding, going there like that, in broad daylight, making us think he was going to work... turning around to see if he's being followed, almost running in his impatience to indulge that, that vice... coming out casting disquiet looks on all sides, coming home as though nothing had happened, like a good citizen, a good paterfamilias, working like everyone else, by the sweat of his brow, like everybody, everywhere, in offices, in factories, in the mines, in the fields... whereas he tried to steal away, he fled, cowering... and once there, nobody any the wiser, alone... for himself, alone... time passes but time is short, one must tear oneself away from that, leave this forbidden fruit, interrupt this sensual pleasure... in broad daylight, on a working day, isn't that shameful? who ever heard of such a thing... wasting his strength, coming out of there exhausted, in a daze, incapable of getting on his feet again, obliged to drop down beside the old women, pensioners, vacuous mothers on the benches, beside the lawns... Not a word to us, of course, when he finally comes in, with a busy look... Did anyone telephone? Show me the mail...

And then, between themselves, between people of the same rank, of the same species, between old hedonists, old pleasure-seekers, they gradually grow confidential, they unburden themselves... moist lips of old gourmets... Yes, I know her... Perfection. Superb. But you know there exists in the Prado, in Rome, in Basel, in Berlin..., I don't know whether you noticed her... raising his heavy body, walking toward the middle of the room, extending his leg, a real model

87

strutting in a dressmaker's salon... If you knew...
right here, in this curve, in this line... he brings his
hand up the length of his thigh, of his hip... here, you
see, on the extended right leg, there, like that... his
lips make a repulsive sound, a kiss smacks on the ends
of his fingers.... I shan't say more. Absolutely marvelous! I stood looking at her for hours. I couldn't tear
myself away from her. Egyptian, yes, on the left, right
next to the window. That alone is worth the journey.

But doesn't it seem as though little by little his voice
were becoming hoarse, forced... he has finally noticed,
he has remembered that we are there... No, that would
be too perfect, he's much too excited, there's nothing
you can do, for him to come to himself, come to us
again, extreme measures must be taken... Open the
door softly, go down silently one after the other...
And right away... you should see him, it's a delectable
sight, caught red-handed, caught in the act, still button-
ing up all excited, pulling himself together, turning toward us, coughing to gain time, to gain self-assurance...
—So, you've come downstairs again? Not sleepy?
True enough, it was a bit early to go to bed... in spite
of being tired... By the way, what about that fishing-
trip? And that hike?... How did they go?... A
second later he has recovered his memory, he has recalled the code, all the signs that we alone know are
present in his voice, in his intonation... not even in
them... waves which we alone can catch, without anything appearing on the outside, are transmitted directly

to us... —Well yes, we had a good time. A nice day. Very nice... That's fine... It's a pleasure to see that he has so quickly recovered his senses, that nothing has been lost, and that there is even distinct progress. Suddenly, this time, it's complete surrender. No question of limiting ourselves, of relying only on the invisible waves, or even on intonations. Did you hear that?... Of course. What a question!... "Hike." No less. Astonishing how fear sometimes makes you more keen, inventive, rejecting "walk" in a flash and seizing upon that: hike. Even dragging it out a bit: hi-i-ke. Running up that white flag. Very good, that. Here's something that deserves encouragement. A pat on the fawning back. Bravo. Good dog... Excellent, that hi-i-ke. Terrific. Damned well done...

So far so good. There was no need to take action, to waste time, as formerly, when he was still so imprudent, when he kept on, as though unaware of our presence, unbosoming himself, perfectly free and easy, quite shamelessly, so excited, incapable of stopping, as modesty, simple decency demand... when that obliged us, finally to obtain surrender, to sit over to one side, just anywhere in a corner, and to stay there, without budging, above all without taking part, without speaking, not a word, seeming to be only half-listening, leafing through or even reading a magazine or a book...

But it's not possible that he could be taken in... It's amusing to watch how he tries to rise above, to lift his head as high as possible above what issues, secreted by us, from this stratus of noxious gas that emanates from our motionless presence, from our silence... thickens, spreads, little by little rises up to him... He sits up very straight, a little cock on its spurs, a little marquis on his high heels, he stretches to take a breath of fresh air, as though he were the equal of the other, his innocent companion, he talks with vivacity like him, he laughs, he holds out his hand, he is going to stroke the rough flanks of the animal... the silken covers of art books... one quite like the other, on the same level... it's so touching... what do you know, he too, just like the other, secure among the glazed percales, the sweet-peas, the meadows, the ponies... both so far from where we are, from the dank, dark back-courtyards where he used to play with us...

He nods his head, he is thinking, he replies... —Yes, I believe you are right. Zapotec, probably. Yes, that's true, from this angle... But the words that he does his utmost to pronounce must be thrown harder and harder to make them go through the thickness that is slowly accumulating... the words come out distorted, weakened, trembling, they drift away, they have lost their sheen, they are dull, gray, poor soiled words, dusty, as though covered with plaster, with cement... The other stretches out his hand toward the animal... is about to touch it... he must be restrained, stopped, don't call out... watch out, don't touch it, it's danger-ous, don't you feel anything?... while that uncon-scious fellow... deaf, insensitive... very calmly lays his hand on it, turns it slowly around to get a better view of it... —There, look how the light brings out that line... very lovely... It makes me think...

His words, as though surrounded only by the purest

90

air, meeting with no resistance rush forward... not the slightest deviation, distortion, trembling, defilement, sparkling with cleanliness, his words rush forward directly toward their target: And you over there, have you nothing to say? How do you like it? What do you think of it?

Who, me? What I think of it? The miserable creature dazzled by the light that suddenly floods the hovel in which she is sequestered raises herself up with difficulty... she hardly articulates: Me? You're speaking to me?... Yes, to you. Of course. You said nothing. I would like to know what you think of it... To me, as you would to an equal?... Yes, as to a human being like any other. Equally worthy of the same respect...

Her red-faced torturer, his eyes popping, does his utmost to come up with a mealy-mouthed smile on his face... Why yes, it's true, you said nothing... Go on, my dear, if you dare... try...

And why shouldn't I try? Ah, but the fact is we are no longer alone, my poor friend, I am protected... You see, a number of decent people have mixed in... It's a real miracle, this unexpected intervention, this sudden release... Your head reels, it's the outdoor air... you feel as though you were intoxicated... What I think of it? I? You'll excuse me but really how could I let pass such an opportunity?... And suddenly going through a transformation. Acquiring assurance. Her voice very calm... Well, I myself, I think... the tone perhaps a bit too sure, unanswerable... still bearing the too visible traces of long years of rebuffs, or humiliations... Well, personally, I'm obliged to say that it reminds me of Crete. Of Cretan sculpture... And rising, taking leave with perfect ease of manner, while the tyrant, clutching the arms of his chair to keep from grabbing the impudent girl, from hitting her... congested, panting, extends his head as though to bite: Of what?

Not bad. It was a fine spectacle. They all realized it. He'll never get over it. "That reminds me of Cretan sculpture." Like that. All at once. Where did you get that?... No matter, it was what was needed. Now, having made this effort—for just the same it took a great display of force to come out with that— now we can have a little fun... You still look quite pale... come on, relax... Look... Oh, what's that? That's fantastic, hey there, hand it to me... That's a scream.

Laughter... aimless, targetless, spreads out freely in the void that surrounds them... innocent spurts, childish explosions... again and again... And then nothing more... Across the table the nice frank eyes look into his... I wonder why... —Why what? —I wonder why Cretan sculpture... the large hand slowly turns the animal around... Cretan sculpture... how strange...

—Strange. Yes. Really. Strange... the shaky partition inside him is swaying, it is going to give way... Strange, you're right, I think so too... Strange to have thought of that... Why Cretan, in fact? Why not Chinese? Chaldean? Greek? Byzantine? Egyptian? African? Why?... It bears down, it is going to sweep away everything... impossible to stop it... Why? Because they generally say everything that comes into their heads to prove... to belie what they know I think of their incurable laziness, of their ignorance... It is mounting in him, boiling up, his voice is rising... To bowl me over... He is panting... to... to... but they don't give a rap about all that... He sweeps the walls with a broad gesture of his outspread hand, with the back of his hand he gives a smack on the animal's muzzle... All that, you understand... and more... everything, everything, everything... they systematically destroy, they burn, they blow up...

The other stretches out his arm as though to protect himself, to repulse him... —Not at all, see here, what will you invent next... Calm yourself... You know, after all, that was perhaps not as wrong as it seemed at first glance... Strictly speaking one might have... And right away inside him the gigantic waves subside... When I come to think about it, it seems to me that there have been in Crete certain statues... not well known, it's true... And the tumult starts up again... —Not well known! And do you believe that they precisely, they who have never in their lives looked... —Well, once was enough... it's enough to have been struck one single time... and it just happened that that was the right one... It's enough to have noticed it once by chance and to have made the connection. Fools rush in...

Calm... How calm everything is... moonbeams give to the becalmed waters the aspect of a silver lake... No postcard shows a more beautiful view than the one that is now outlined in him... His voice is gentle, made weak with emotion... —Fools rush in... And then, do we really know them? They are the ones we know least well... We are too prejudiced... —That's true, you're not indulgent enough. We don't know what they're really like. You less than anybody... that's natural. They may be quite different from what you think. Perhaps you would be surprised...

The survivor brought back to life and carried on a stretcher, whose wounds have been dressed, who has been given injections to calm him, now, far from storms, from glaciers, from crevasses, from high walls of sheer rock, from the dead and dying, stretched out between smooth sheets... while the nurses who tuck him in bend over him their pure, serene faces, their white caps, stretches himself, gently sighs, falls asleep...

Everything in the house is sleeping. The sweet-peas are leaning from the old vases. On the spacious, soft easy-chairs the percales are wrinkled with delightful abandon... the door upstairs opens slowly... and there they are... they come down in silence... the floor cracked... they stop, hold one finger in front of their lips, their mischievous dimples deepen, their fresh mouths open halfway... they are advancing... toward what? what are they doing?... He is waiting... But already before they approach, his joy announces what they are about to... yes, it's possible... Yes, it's sure... they advance toward that... toward that sculpture left there, on the low table... they lift it... but he's not afraid... their gestures are full of precaution, of reverence... they hold it at arm's length, they turn it around... but there's nothing to fear... they are whispering... Yes, you see... I've thought it for a long time... No doubt. Look at that line. Admit I was right. Cretan. That's what it is... Unknown delights. It must be something like that which we call happiness...

But watch out, they're going to turn around... He must clear out, above all they must hear nothing, they must not know that he is there spying on them... they must not feel his eyes upon them... A repugnant contact which would make them shrivel up, harden... From now on there's nothing they wouldn't do to force him to put it away, to hide it in the depths of his memory... to crush this idyllic vision, this celestial apparition born of his senile desires, of his miserable dissolute imagination... Never again the slightest suspicion of interest, even out of politeness, even in the presence of strangers... Cretan sculpture, even said to flout him, to show how easy it is, if they feel like it, to beat him on his own ground... Cretan sculpture, even taken at random and dropped there out of pure derision, would seem to him like a charming bit of teasing, a delicious tickling, a caress, beside the order to which they were going to subject him from now on, without ever giving in.

No mark of respect on the part of all the innocents in the world could ever again move them, disarm them... Even by approaching them, seated there saying nothing in a corner, by humbly coming to beg, bearing in his arms, holding out to place on their knees... this color reproduction... Look... You rarely see them as good as this... What do you think of it? you would only get that little gesture of brushing it aside... —Oh, as for me, you know... with one of those laughs that give you the shivers... personally, things like that, I don't see them. I'm a Daltonian myself, you know... —What? Daltonian! What's that you're saying? What won't you invent? You're kidding us!

And the gentle innocent with the smooth, pink face of a priest who has consoled countless afflicted... there's no brute, however hardened who, if treated kindly, with great gentleness... intercedes... —Don't get excited... You won't succeed like that... But you know, my dear child, that's not a reason. Daltonism doesn't prevent anything. A transposition takes place. There are painters who are Daltonians... But no amount of long-suffering, of patience can save these fallen, lost souls, can lead this one, which is irretrievable, if only for a few seconds, back to the straight and narrow path. —Well, you know, personally, Daltonian or not, painting means nothing to me. Sculpture either, for that matter. Nor art in general. To be quite frank: Art with a capital A. The Art that Papa respects, adores. It can be the result of having been dragged to museums... Thank goodness, I never set foot in them anymore... The hoary head is wagging, from the candid eyes there radiate indulgence, pity... —It's very sad, my poor child, to hear you talk like that... You are depriving yourself of great joys... You distress your poor papa... who meant well... who wanted to give... to share... He may have been clumsy, but believe me, there are many who in your place... —Oh yes, many, there are lots of papa's boys... He was one himself... You never heard him... Go ahead, do your act for him, tell it, it's so edifying, that initiation to which, from generation unto generation, all the boys in your family were subjected... even the girls were not spared... Tell about the shock, the first time, when you encountered, what was it again? Not the smile of the Mona Lisa, that one was for Grandpa... Not the Venus de Milo, that was still the preceding generation... Go ahead, tell it, don't make us beg you, it's not shyness however that chokes you people... go on, tell it... Ah, you see, sir, how stubborn he is... You know, if you don't tell it, I'm going to tell it for you... It was Fragonard, eh, the first shock? Fragonard or Watteau, eh? you little rascal, already rakish and voluptuous at that age...

And that hasn't changed, believe me. It's only grown worse, above all recently... with the decrease in activity... the escapades are closer together, last longer... Do you believe then that nobody knows about it? And I assure you that we would be willing to look the other way, everybody is free, after all, do we ourselves ask him to go into ecstasies over that comic-strip exhibition... marvellous, by the way... we know perfectly well that he would sneer, "insulting to our feelings"... The fact is they're pitiless, they are... not at all compassionate... very offhanded and without consideration... They are so sure that they're on the right side, supported by all the most respected, the ones who continue to practice the official cult, by all the faithful who never fail, on feast days, to go with their families to make their devotions in the art galleries, in the museums... And here in a hitherto honorable family, this misfortune occurs... Whence? How? during his sleepless nights he wonders... Whence such a marked propensity for vulgarity, for platitudes?...

MORTAL BLAST, DEATH RAY. Words that come from them, among the ones to be seen printed in big black letters above their comic strips, rise up, float inside him, pass back and forth... and then nothing more... nothing but a rather agreeable torpor... a daze...

Opposite him the heavy man with the pink face of a country gentleman is motionless, silent, as though dozing... What is that dirty-gray statuette in rough stone doing here, the one of a clumsy, dumpy animal, with a short snout, with ears like wheels, like tires... that's not where it belongs, on this low table... Nor over there, on the mantelpiece where it replaced... something had to be put there... the marble clock with the broken pendulum... It should have remained in the cellar with the broken chairs, the old trunks, the old pots, the chipped china pitchers and bowls... Why hadn't he brought up instead the little mermaid, given him long ago... by whom?... so delicate to the touch... delicate to the eye which roves at will the length of her milky curves... But the elongated form of the alabaster tiger with the golden highlights would perhaps go still better with the line and color of the mantelpiece, with the faded shades of the sheafs and bouquets printed on the curtains, on the glazed percale slipcovers, on the old porcelain vases from which are leaning the lavender, pink and white flowers of the sweet-peas...

He gives a start, he sits up, he knocks, he calls out... they should un-nail the top, displace the slab... they should release him, they should let him out... Just for a few seconds more... just one single time...

He refrains from running along the quais, on the garden walks, he goes through the great gate of the old palace as slowly as possible, climbs the huge stair-case, crosses the succession of rooms in which stand, in which lie whitish forms... But over there, near the window... still in the same place... there it is... secure in its glass case...

No impatience. Be calm. With her nothing is ever gratuitous... she only vouchsafes herself to the most deserving... one must assemble all the strength that remains, not divert a single particle... one must tauten... open up... create a vacuum in oneself... for her again as before to let radiate, flow, run over...

They open the door, they go down, they enter... The two old men are seated opposite each other, sunk in their armchairs, their still half-filled glasses set in front of them on the low table. Look at this one: he is still holding his pipe tight between his teeth... And this stone animal... What's it doing there? What is it? A rhinoceros? A puma? No, look at its ears. It is more likely a mythical animal... A sacred object which probably was used by a certain cult... What cult? How can one find out what it might have represented for them... They raise, turn, palpate... these remains...

—Don't you sometimes have the impression that it's finished, all that... Dead. A dead world. We are the inhabitants of Pompeii entombed under the ashes. We are mummies in their sarcophagi. Buried with their everyday objects... The other sits up in his armchair, leans forward... —Come, come, what are you talking about?... What are you going to invent now? How can you let yourself be impressed, affected by such childishness? Revolts of surfeited adolescents... They'll get over it.

Do you hear him? Do you hear what your friend says? What your brother, your double, is saying...

Look at him, he's a mirror in which you should be able to recognize yourself... look at this somewhat too pink, somewhat too smooth face, steeped for so many hours, during so many years, in quietude, in security, in the gorged contentment of meditation... when hat in hand, all the forbidden objects, canes, umbrellas, left in the checkroom... after having patiently stood in line to get in, you slowly slip in among the true believers, you stop, you stand congealed... Ah, naturally, we were a bit congested... even during the week, even at less crowded hours... but I didn't have the patience to wait... I wanted at least to enter into a first contact... But I'll go back... I've already been twice... Don't you think that what dominates all the rest, what puts everything in the shade... I should say so... It's exquisite. You could get down on your knees in front of it...

—But what's the matter with them? What are they doing now up there? What is the matter with them that they should be laughing like that? —What do you think is the matter with them? They're having fun, that's all... that's normal... Remember when, once we got started...

No, what were we thinking of? He your double, your very image? But we didn't think that... not really... it was a joke... to tease you... He your reflection in the mirror, that half-deaf blunderbuss uttering those platitudes in that big hearty voice of his... as if that could reassure you... keep you from retracting, from shivering... when between you and him, when between you and all the marvellous things scattered throughout the world, insinuating itself, wafted down from above, from our rooms, is this whiff of tart wind... of fresh air... Look at him, he's wriggling in his chair, he raises his hand to enforce silence... he lifts his head impatiently... he sits up straight, pricks up his ears... —No... Listen...

The dose must be increased... Increased? Who said increase? Who, even in an inaudible language, even talking to himself, would have committed the imprudence to say "increase"? Who among them doesn't know that this laughter, to be effective, should be absolute innocence, absolute spontaneity... an uprush of living waters, cooing, chirping... irrepressible... how do you restrain it, restrain yourself, when it's so funny, so screamingly funny... Not so loud, they'll hear you... not so loud, see here, they can hear you downstairs... You're going to disturb them... hands in front of their mouths, they burst out laughing... again and again... oh how can you stop once you get started... now almost nothing is needed, a gesture, a harmless word, and the explosions multiply, propagate, spread... what can be more contagious, isn't it so? when the terrain is propitious, and it is... fed by unconcern, childish instability, frivolity...

What fears, rancors, what dubious desires, what miasmas coming from below and infiltrating here could reach them... What's it all about? What is that? I don't understand a thing about it, not a thing. Do you?... I don't either, naturally... Oh look... it's too funny... the laughter spreads... it's a scream... oh hand it here... pass it on, pass and re-pass, again and again... just under the surface, insinuating itself, exploding all of a sudden, then becoming silent, proceeding underneath... subterranean water... and then it spurts up, rises in a geyser, very high, too high... Oh watch out, you're going to disturb them... they thought we had gone to bed... and it starts up again... that we were... impossible to finish... they're choked with giggling... Oh be quiet, I'm exhausted, be quiet, you wear me out... isn't he silly... aren't we idiotic... We *are* idiotic... I ask you: what did I say this time that was so screamingly funny? —acting the fool, assuming the dismayed expression of an old student monitor... Ssh, ssh... behave yourselves... How old are you anyway? How old... Oh, help... oh stop, I beg of you... stop... don't you hear? look at the knob... ha, ha, what knob? no, this time, that's going too far... the outbursts follow one another uninterruptedly... The doorknob, stupid... it's turning, somebody knocked... Who's there?

The big animal crouching in the back of its lair has been smoked out, it has come out... open the door, let it in... But look, the dose was too strong, it falls down, its big bulbous eyes are dimmed, it's going to pass out... And we who thought that it would still have the strength to bite, that we'd never get the better of it... It's frailer than it seems... So then, what's the matter? What on earth is the matter? What happened? That annoyed you considerably, eh? You can't stand that giggling... you feel like biting the way you always do whenever somebody teases you a bit... No? Not bite? Really? You're not cross? Well I declare, there's been a misdeal, he was exchanged in infancy, as our storybooks used to say... he's not the same... No, it's he, it's he all right, I recognize him. I know him like my own pocket... It's true that he would have bitten if he had still had the strength to do it... If we hadn't taken all the time that was needed for him to come crawling to beg for grace... for him to give proof of his innocence...

Your laughing? What laughing? I didn't hear anything. I just heard some noise... You're not in bed yet? If you knew how I'd like to be in your place... But there's nothing to be done about it, I must go back down there...

She lays her hand on his bent back... you don't hit a man when he's down... she smiles at him, she kisses him on the cheek... There now, keep up your courage a little longer. It won't be long now... So have no more fear, peace has been concluded... you are forgiven... Like a child who has come up to his mother to get a kiss, then goes back, reassured, to play with his little friends, he is going to go back downstairs... He makes us a little sign with his hand, a little pert, boyish sign, he has a mischievous, pitiable, touching smile put awkwardly, a bit askew, on his distended face, bloated with age...

—Enough now. That's enough. It's time to go to bed, we've been acting like children, playing, long enough... —Enough? Really? Enough? —Yes, enough. He has given sufficient proof. —What proof? —Everybody here saw it. Everybody saw him arrive, carrying the dead animal. Everybody saw him lay this offering at our feet. A great sacrifice, you know that. No angel came to stay his hand. He killed it. He brought it and he threw it there. —I saw no such thing. You take your desires for reality.

—No, I saw him; for a moment I myself felt that he was about to give in... the flesh is weak... however much he struggled, however much he held the living animal close and warm in his arms, tried at all cost to save it, he couldn't resist our repeated warning shots... Finally he turned away from it, he abandoned it, uncared for, he let it die, and then he seized it and brought it here... You saw him, don't say no... Whom are you trying to bluff? Where do you think you are? Whom do you hope to fool? Who did not see, when he came in, that he was holding the lifeless animal in his arms? They remain silent... Ah, you see, everybody here saw it. He set it down before us and he said: There. I have obeyed. I have brought it to you. You can see for yourself, it is quite dead. You can turn it

over and over. It is a carcass. A poor piece of
refuse.... You heard him? —Yes. Everybody heard
him clearly; he said that. But we should have ques-
tioned him. Intentions are what matter. We should
have asked him why he did it. —Ask him? Why, we
did ask him. —Who? —I did. At the moment when
he set it down here, on the floor, I said to him: That's
good, that's very good, but it's not the first time. One
thing is certain, you won't be caught again using it
against us. You are cured of that. It is not big enough
to defend you... Too frail, too vulnerable... Just
enough to impress the poor devils that we were, when
we were prisoners, locked up down there with you, at
your mercy. But there are all the others... He asked,
coward, traitor that he is: What others? I burst out
laughing... Come, come, don't play-act, come, come,
go downstairs, go join your friend, go talk to him about
your secret expeditions, far from our impious eyes...
relish... that line... of the thigh... that movement...
finer than anything I saw in Rome, in Berlin.. But he
went on his knees... Don't tell me that you haven't
seen it... he said clearly, he said out loud quite in-
telligibly: No, that's finished. No more thighs, arms,
lines, forms, colors, no more of all that... if only you
would accept... —Yes, it was awful, that icy gaze
you turned on him, when you said: If we would accept
what?... He was slightly trembling, he threw his arms
around my knees, tears were streaming down his face:
If you would accept me, me, if you would not reject
me... I am ready to sacrifice everything... no more
escapades, no more betrayals, never again any move-

106

ments of revolt, of aggression, if you would keep me with you... never go away as you did a while ago, never do that again...

What do you mean that? He turned away, poor thing... What do you mean that? He didn't dare say what, he knew it was dangerous, these are things that— even at the point we had arrived at—it's wiser not to touch... to show to what extent he had become like us, quite ready, if we accepted him, to take part in our games, he settled for that mischievous gesture, that poor, boyish smile... Did you see it? I couldn't bear it, I kissed him... Okay, get up, go on downstairs. You've understood, that's all that's needed. Go now, the outsider downstairs is waiting for you... His eyes shone with joy when I said that: The outsider, the intruder downstairs must be surprised... I gave him a pat on the shoulder and he looked away to hide his tears of gratitude, of tenderness... Hurry up, go on down, your visitor must be wondering what is happening, what you are doing, shut in with us up here...

—You didn't go and scold them, I hope? Personally, you know, they don't disturb me... —Scold? Me? Them? Scold! Ah, a lot they would care. That would be something. It's been a long time since I had the right to say a word. They are the ones who lay down the law. Somebody said that at present parents treat their offspring like distinguished guests... with infinite consideration... You walk on tiptoe, you shrink in size, you feel rewarded when they deign to show forbearance... But then you must have deserved it. Nothing is overlooked... not so much as that... He makes a clacking sound with his thumbnail against his teeth... and believe me, there are no limits. The more you give in to them, the more exigent they become...

The other starts to cough slightly... the air he is obliged to breathe upsets him... —I can't say anything to you about that, myself, you know... Those are matters about which I haven't the slightest experience. Probably paternity, like marriage, for it to work, one must have a vocation for it. I didn't have it, which I realized very early...

And then his hand stretches out, caresses the stone animal on the low table between them... His face relaxes... His eyes grow misty...

But all at once: Listen... like a slap on the back, tears him from his trance... He sits up straight: What's the matter now? What is it? —There's something... —Ah, it's still that? It's that laughter?... —Well, not exactly the laughter... in itself the laughter is nothing... —No, nothing, that's true... I'm glad to hear you say it... —It's nothing in itself, but there is in it... I know that it's quite unreasonable... that it's insane... —Yes, insane, it is that. And you take pleasure in it, you wallow in it, you don't want to leave it... What a loss of time... What a waste of energy... When there's nothing. Absolutely nothing. You're in hot pursuit of nothing. So much wind. So much void. You are fighting against nothing. He leans forward, all at once with the look of a mature man, rich in experience, speaking to an adolescent: Nothing, you understand. All you would need to do would be that... his large hand sweeps through the air... and there would be nothing more: kids' laughter. They are having fun. Period. Kids—having fun. Nothing else. It *can't* be anything else. You should refuse to let it be anything else. This laughter is what you make of it. It'll be what you want. I assure you, I don't understand you. He turns toward the window as though he were calling for help... Send out a call to arms, assemble, question thousands of wholesome, normal people, there won't be one among them, do you hear me, who won't tell you that that doesn't hold water, that it is of no interest... Really none... It's ridiculous, exhausting... Look here, answer me rather... This at least is worth thinking about... How, after having adored... you remember... with such exclusive passion... all the honey-colored gods, all the daughters of the golden number, we suddenly took it into our heads... we saw that there was there... in that...

He nods like a good boy, he lets himself be docilely dragged along, his moist little hand held tight in the strong grip...

He stops and remains exposed to the delicate caresses of the golden rays that radiate from the polished marbles, from their swollen lines, gorged with security, with quiet content...

He himself gorged, pacified, he feels overcome by a delightful numbness. He hears, strangely reverberating, as though coming from very far off, a metallic voice with the peremptory intonations of a grown-up.

His heavy head like a movable doll's head is hanging, swaying, as though attached to his torso by a flexible wire... Yes, you are right, it is astonishing... for so many centuries... such an eclipse in taste, in *goût*...*

Goût? Goût, really? Did we hear right? *Goût.* Yes, *goût*... the puckered, ludicrously rounded mouth let that drop: perfectly round, slippery... *goût*... Really, let's have a good laugh. It's enough to split your sides.

He wakes up with a start... —It was a slip of the tongue, I don't know what came over me... I was somewhere else... You know perfectly well, it's not a question of that. —Not of that? perfectly smooth and round, glossy, perfumed, sweet-peas, old vases and glazed percale, pre-Columbian sculpture with its pure, delightfully naïve and skillful lines?... Well-bred people know at first glance where they are... the slightest error and they bristle, they turn away, heavens, they stop their noses... what horrible promiscuity, into what company have we fallen... But it's true that it was a mistake on your part to use that word... Even for you "*goût*" is dubious... it's one of those words... like "distinction"... that could be used to make up charm-

* *Translator's note:* as frequently happens during esthetic discussion, here the two friends achieve greater understanding through introduction of a French word.

110

ing riddles: What is the word which shows right away that the person who uses it is lacking in what the word stands for? Do you give up? Well, it's the word *goût,* ha, ha... —That'll do. Stop your sneering. Who do you take me for? Why this play-acting? You know perfectly well that it has nothing to do with that. —With what, then?... with an idiotic look, swinging back and forth, one finger in her mouth... Tell us... He shouts: It's a matter of strength, boldness, breakthrough, breach, explosion... No matter where... how... a force of attack, a power of destruction... everywhere and always... and in modern art... it can be called whatever you like... op art, pop art... I am quite ready to yield... but it should be art, real art...

Real? Art? Better and better. Art. From Charybdis to Scylla. Art. Ah, Ah, Ah... Art, his mouth wide open to let forth this big balloon blown up with admiration, with veneration... Straight ahead, not batting an eye... wearing the livery handed down from father to son... trained in early youth in the service of the Masters... proud to show the impressed lower classes who follow him through the large paneled rooms of the palaces, between the high windows giving onto gardens, the brilliant likenesses relating the great deeds of these heroic warriors, of these glorious conquerors, of these martyred saints of the faith...

All those who have deserved to occupy here the place conferred upon them by their prerogatives of divine right, the virtues that derive from their noble birth, receive from him the same marks of respect, the same care...

And we, who are called upon to succeed him, we whose humble origin has destined us, like him, for subordinate roles, for easy humble tasks, we must learn to be content with, to rejoice in our modest estate... we must feel gratified when the great of this world deign to let fall upon us, who are faithfully attached to them, a little of their radiance...

But these scamps, this devilish breed, even if you educate them, try everything... kindness, force... preach a good example... let nothing pass, keep constant watch on them, they have a perverted inclination to sully, to sack... Excuse me... advancing humbly, cap in hand... no matter how I punish them, there's nothing you can do... this new generation... —Come, come, pull yourself together, my good man, I know you, I appreciate your devotion, don't let yourself get into such a state, don't scold them too much, you'll see, they'll outgrow it... they don't know what they're doing... —Oh, shrunken, humility seeping from every pore... oh, when I think of what they dared... with regard to something so sacred... after so many reprimands, so many recommendations... Not to touch... to dust and polish with infinite precaution... what liberties they took... But it was against me, those malicious, vicious little brats wanted to flout me, to cover me with shame... —Calm yourself, my good man, is it really so serious as that? —Yes, it's very serious... —But what is it? What on earth did they do? —They... it's simply atrocious... they amused themselves, like the good-for-nothings that they are, the way kids tie a tin can to a cat's tail... they took that kind of corrugated paper you find, with all due respect, on the bottom of cookie, chocolate boxes, and they manufactured... a collar, a ruff, which they put around the neck of this statue... a mythical animal... a sort of puma... I saw it one morning... I cried out, I called them and they came running, displaying their smiling faces, letting out their exasperating little titters... I could hardly speak, I pointed a finger at the object... Who? Which one of you did that? And they looked at one another while refraining from bursting out laughing: Who? You? Or you?

And then they formed a semi-circle in front of me and one of them stepping forward a little said to me in a provocative tone: It was all of us. All together. This ruff is the product of a collective effort. Collective effort. Absolutely. And pushing me aside, they went to the mantelpiece, in spite of my entreaties, my cries, they took in their hands and carried, set here, belly up... Don't you think it's better like that? No? But have no fear, we won't break it... they patted it... Admit it's nicer in this position... and that ruff suits it marvellously... We made that, just like that, in a moment of inspiration... with just anything, every sort of material can be used... today even your famous masters, isn't it true, do not disdain the lowliness of lead, when they feel like it... Only we never try to change it into pure gold, we play around a bit, that's all... Tear that off if you want, look, I'll take it off, don't worry... But you'll admit that suited it, you'll admit that dressed it up... there is something a bit mournful, a bit clumsy about it, that lightened it up a bit, that gave it a sort of something...

Then I came to my senses, I took them by the scruff of the neck, I shook them... Poor little old graybeards, abject imitators, docile grandsons of the ones who fifty years ago were painting on mustaches, yes, you know that perfectly well... believing that they were breaking entirely with everything, making a clean sweep of everything... and we know how since... come on, skedaddle, get to bed...

And they went upstairs without a word, they shut themselves in up there... I believed I had crushed them, I thought I had reduced them to nothing... and then the laughter started up again... those long peals of laughter like thin lashes that sting and coil up...

No really, it's too funny, did you hear that? The Mona Lisa... a mustache on the Mona Lisa... They're still back with that, making their chronological lists, their wretched order of priority to serve the insatiable self-esteem of their masters, of the "creators"... A mustache on the Mona Lisa... That's true, nobody had thought of it, bravo, we're delighted... All that is finished, my poor dear, honor rolls, hierarchies... precursors that way... this way the imitators... that way the great, this way the little fellows... As for mustaches, that was fine, we regret that we weren't there to take part, to see what kind of face you made... Really, that's idiotic, I feel sorry for him... an entire life pent-up, steeped in humility, never daring to make so bold... Take that, for instance... tearing up the cookie box, letting the cookies drop on the floor, stepping on the pieces, tearing out the corrugated paper, folding it... The laughter stops, the faces grow serious... Hey, hand it to me, I've got an idea... or rather no, it's too small, a cardboard box would do better... they look around them... that, why not, and not around its neck, rather around its snout, or else no, around its belly... lower... and it should be seated, that'll look like a ballet skirt... all at once I'm beginning to like it... that gives it an air... a manner... that's a dirty word... Look how pale he grew, that makes him faint... it's so vulgar, isn't it? so lowdown... But don't look so desperate, here, we're giving it back, we're giving you back your rattle, look, it hasn't its pretty belt any more, its handsome collar... too bad, that was so becoming to it... there, calm yourself, we are tearing it up, we're throwing it away... We, gentlemen, you know, we have no author's vanity, we are not trying to manufacture rare objects, collection pieces... no aim at wealth, at fame, either near or far... We are detached, very pure. All equals. All geniuses... You too, you know, are a genius... you too, why not? if only you wanted to be... You too...

Their firm palms grip his hands... Come, have a little fun, the way we do, stand up, give yourself a good stretching, get rid of that numbness... But watch out, he has escaped, look at him, he's crouching behind his friend's armchair... What are you doing there? You're hiding, you're as afraid as all that? See here, come out of there... he lets himself be taken hold of, pulled, he nods his head without speaking... a smile spreads across his old idiot's smooth face... You'll see, we'll have fun, we'll dance... listen, that'll be good for you, we'll have amateur theatricals... let yourself go... open your sluices, break down your barriers, sit up straight after all, leap, spurt... they pat him on the chest, on the forehead... there are "treasures" in there, "undreamed-of wealth," as you would say... as in us, as in everybody... You don't think so? There's nothing to be done about it? You don't want to? That's all you have to say? You prefer to remain flopped down there, as heavy and lifeless as this animal... look at it... See here, take it, go carry it back to the mantelpiece, that's where it belongs... he leans over, he takes it in his hands... and they push him... A little less precaution, don't look as if you were carrying the holy oils, the holy sacrament... there... it's all right where it is... And now you're going to see... but look how stiff he is, how he has shrunk, hardened... all that should be allowed to soak... in unconcern, in free-and-easiness... You have been released, you are free, understand that... no more lords and masters, no more devotional images, the master is you, you alone are at the helm, you and your sovereign gesture... There's nothing more to fear, no more judges, no more laws... It's pitiful to see what so many years, an entire life passed in submission, in devotion, have made of you, never allowing you even in thought, so much as that... watch what we do... it's so easy...

"Easy"... look how he retracts, the word frightens him... one of their watch-your-step words, one of their sheep-dog words that make them immediately clear out, run and take refuge huddled up to one another in the fold... Easy. Yes. But that mustn't frighten you anymore. Easy, and why not? So much the better, it's delightful, no more need to be subjected to tests, failures, despair, renunciations, trembling recommencings, deadly sweats, flagellations, prosternations, long hours passed in waiting for a sign, however weak, proving that you have been chosen... All are chosen. All are called. There will never again be any eliminations, any exclusions... stand up, stretch your stiff legs, now don't be afraid...

He casts the look of an embarrassed child asked to recite his poem before the assembled family at the motionless friend sunk in his easy chair... Don't look at him, forget him, forget everything... Come... take off these cumbersome clothes... do like us... we'll amuse ourselves all together... He lifts himself up with effort... But what is it? What is it you want to do? Is it a play? Is it a ballet? How do you expect me... Oh, what does he want now? It's really enough to get discouraged... No, we must have a little more patience... It hasn't got a name, you understand... No more names, no more labels, no more definitions...

117

it is what it will become, nobody knows, nobody wants to know... throw yourself into it recklessly, lost to the world... Lost, that's it, lost with no return, forgotten, unknown, out of sight, out of mind... in empty, weightless space... he feels that his big heavy body... Who said that? Who said big? Who said body? Who said heavy? Where do these words come from? They are on me. They are plastered on me... the words cover me... pull them off... They drag him away, they make him turn, they make him lie down, get up, the big heavy mass, the pachyderm, the elephant starts to dance...

He looks laughingly at those old words that have come off him, he tramples on them... That's what has been clinging to me all my life... big heavy body... I'm no longer afraid... look what I do with them... but as he becomes more and more carried away by the movement, that too comes off him, scales that peel off the skin of a convalescing scarlet-fever patient... There's no more "look," no more "I," no more "do"...

Nothing except what now, in him, through him, between them and him, is propelling, circulating, they are one, they are like the coils of a serpent that rears up, sways, crawls, climbs on the furniture, on the staircase, rolls into a ball, drops down lackadaisically, unrolls, stretches, shoots out to one side then to the other... water is running from the overturned vases... a flower held erect in his hand like a candle is swinging to and fro... Falling breathless into his chair he raises his head and sees their smiling faces leaning over him...

118

You see what you make me do... You make me do such crazy things...

Thumb and forefinger pressing against the corners of his closed eyelids, as though to think more effectively, the friend seated opposite on the other side of the low table remains motionless, silent. Immutable. Impregnable. As insensitive as the walls of a fortress to the little waves lapping against them, to the tiny creatures moving about in the ooze of the moat.

—Listen... Now do listen... He removes his hand, he opens his weary eyes—Yes? What's the matter? —I have the impression at times... you're going to laugh, you too... that... that life... excuse me, it's ridiculous... well, what for lack of a better name must be called like that... now life is among them, not here, no longer in that... he flicks a finger against the animal's flank... All that's over. Finished. Soon nothing will remain, everything that appears will disappear right away... destroyed as fast as it is made... perpetual flow... we'll not be able to keep, care for, preserve anything anymore, no more treasures, no more devotional objects like this one, they don't want that anymore... And without them...

—Ah, really, they don't want that anymore? And all that is finished? But how sad that is... he lays his hand on the animal's back and makes it slide over the table toward him... You see, they're through with us... Why, how unfortunate, how awful, and what will

119

become of us, poor things... —Yes, that's truer than you think... leaning across the table, whispering... What will become of us? Yes, what will become of us without them? —Without them? What will become of us? the old friend tosses his head, from his eyes there flows compassion... Excuse me if I hurt your feelings, but I think we'll have to do without them. Alas, we'll have to resign ourselves to that. And he'll laugh best who laughs last. Because we are strong, very strong, what's in there is very strong, it has enormous force... The day they try to destroy that... But that day's not yet here, I think that you give them lots of credit, you make them out more formidable than they are, the poor little duffers will never be up to it...

Hands dug deep in their trousers pockets, caps pulled down over their eyes, cigarette stubs hanging from their lips, they stroll nonchalantly between the auction-blocks, stopping from time to time to listen to the ceaseless ballyhoo, watch with a disgusted pout the repulsive gestures of the slave merchants pushing forward, turning, patting the legs, slapping the flanks... Here, perhaps, I'll admit there's a certain softness in the outline of the thigh, but look at the line of the back... incomparable. All the innocence and all the force of the primitives. A choice specimen. What more can one say? Eyes on the look-out describe a circle, a voice falters... Come now, make up your minds...

But nobody makes a move. Nobody is "up" to it.

All too poor. Too wanting. You can keep it for yourself. Keep that beauty for yourself. Much good it will do you.

He raises his head and suddenly, with a look that he himself is surprised at, with something in him that even before he has spoken forces them to back away, sticking close to one another: Yes. Much good.

Astonishing how that sufficed: that touch in his tone all at once, in spite of himself, that showed them... they can hardly believe it... that he really is detached from them, that he neglects them, that he forgets them, is turned in on himself, contemplating what is there inside him and stating quite naturally with perfect calm, perfect seriousness: Yes. Much good.

And they in turn, in spite of themselves, as though out of contagion, immediately rise up, stand at attention, faces motionless, eyes fixed on him.

Yes. Much good. And above all not add another word. Take advantage of this unhoped-for victory, consolidate his positions. Yes. Much good, you understand. And that will do now. Out you go, make it quick, vanish.

But now it begins to well up, it's rising in him, fills him, inundates him, encountering no more obstacles it is running over, impossible to hold it back, yes, much good, the greatest good that exists here below, those moments of contact, of perfect fusion...

Into their eyes which have started to move again, into their revived faces something has crept... one of them makes a movement toward him, the others gently restrain him... Why not let him speak... It's interesting... —Yes. Interesting, indeed, quite side-splitting, isn't it? Quite side-splitting to have wanted to give you... he's walking up and down in front of them... the best of all I possess... all that nobody can take from you... Yes, side-splitting to treat you as distinguished guests to whom one gives the place of honor, for whom one brings up from the cellar, to whom one serves, one's vintage wines... And still reproaching me with not having been able, with not having known how to give you something even better... and begging you to excuse all the imperfections... doing my utmost, it's really a scream, to hide from you as long as possible... the poor children will find it out soon enough... to hide the graves and only show you the lovely bunches of flowers... and above all to leave you this talisman that will let you at times, for a few seconds, without depending on anybody, exorcise, alone... now what are you smiling at? —Why, we're not smiling... We're listening to you... Yes, to exorcise... excuse me for being grandiloquent... to keep at a respectful distance, death... But you can smile, in fact, you can laugh. You're right. Fool that I was. Pelican. Ready to deprive myself of everything. To sacrifice myself... stepping aside, shriveling up so the little darlings can bloom, take up all the room... May they deign to accept... Is it good enough? Is it well enough presented? Oh, what joy, they don't turn away, on the contrary, look, they're leaning... No? Yes?

They are standing in a semicircle, elbow to elbow close to one another, their faces are motionless, their eyes like glass eyes are staring at him. He moves towards them... Say something after all... after all I'm talking to you... Do you hear me?

He weakly beats their powerful breasts with his little clenched fists, whimpering intonations creep into his voice... I know I am ridiculous, I know that there is nothing to be done with you, that nothing is of any use... Then stepping back, moving away from them, he cries out in a small falsetto voice: But you know, I am not alone. There are people and some of the best... The isolated pedestrian waylaid by toughs on a deserted road turns around, calls out, there are people about, my comrades are there, within earshot, quite near, just beyond the turn in the road, they will come running... There are still a few of us, thank goodness, for whom these things matter... I am not alone in my opinion... All who are still capable of real effort... they are with me... young people of your age for whom I have never lifted a finger, to whom I have never given a thing... and who spontaneously without my asking anything of them... they stand behind me, they support me...

They come nearer to him, they are standing even closer to one another... there is greater harshness, increased gravity in their jaws, in their eyes... Listen to him, listen to his panicky whimpers... You who thought you were unbeatable, so well armed... We frighten you so that you have to place yourself under the protection of the police, now you are calling for help, you are calling for the cops...

—No, it's not that, no, don't believe it... That's not what I wanted... Am I that stupid? Don't I know that you will not let yourselves be impressed, intimidated by arguments of this kind? I just wanted to remind you that I was not alone of my species, not so contemptible, after all, not so mad... I shouldn't have, of course, I don't know what happened to me, it came out in spite of myself...

—In spite of himself... It came out... under the effect, you see, of one of those reflexes conditioned by centuries passed on the side of orthodox, protected, privileged people settled down among their treasures, sitting on their piles... And at the first sign of danger... impossible to keep from doing it... Help me, good people, brave officers to my rescue!... You can't expect me after all to fight against these toughs, we're not alone, thank goodness, the police are there to defend us... A good blackjacking here and there will teach them, those little scoundrels... There's nothing like it for sorting out their ideas...

It seems that we had not yet paid sufficient obeisance to this little marvel. This masterpiece. A pure work of art. Would deserve to figure in a museum. Didn't we hear it proclaimed? Of course we did, and we

124

marched, we paid homage, there was no way of doing otherwise. And then we withdrew. We shut ourselves in our rooms. Even that was not allowed, we should have stayed there all night in ecstasy, we should have grown hoarse singing its praises... That's what he demanded. Eh? Admit, that's what you wanted: to force us to perjure, to demean ourselves... You paled, you went to pieces, when we rose, calm, dignified, distant, when we politely took leave and withdrew in perfect order... But he couldn't stand that, he ran after us... —That's not true, I did not run, I didn't budge from here... —Didn't budge? You didn't come upstairs? You didn't shake the door? —When, then? Much later, when you kept on... —Ah, when I made so bold... what a crime of lèse majesté... when we were having a little fun among ourselves... when we were laughing softly behind the closed door... —Yes, when you made run, trickle down upon us... We were entirely filled with it... We were beginning to suffocate...

—To suffocate? How interesting...

This time it's we who call on all good people, on all wholesome, normal people in the world... on you, sir, who are such a worthy representative, on you who appear—and you are, surely—to be so perfectly balanced... Did you feel anything at all when you heard us laughing that prevented you from breathing? Did you feel discommoded?

125

He turns toward his friend... —Yes, tell them... I beg of you... Admit... It is not possible that you should have felt nothing... Several times you stopped speaking, you listened with an anxious look... Say it...

The friend shakes his head... —I would be happy to support you, I ask nothing better than to stand by you... But however often you called my attention, tried to explain to me... I myself thought... I must confess that that was very innocent laughter, rather droll laughter... giggling, the way people do at that age... you can't stop it after a while... Tossing his head, smiling with a nostalgic, fond look... Yes, young laughter... fresh laughter...

They repeat after him: Young laughter. Fresh laughter. Innocent laughter. Do you hear? Do you hear the voice of reason? Do you hear the voice of wisdom? Innocent laughter. Fresh young laughter.

They repeat the words in rhythm. Like the hammer of boots in the street. Fresh laughter. Young, innocent laughter. Innocent. Innocent. The hammer grows louder, the voices have the raucous notes of command.

It's finally finished, all that madness, all that eccentricity. Order is going to reign. The peace of brave decent people.

There were no longer any limits to the boldness of the troublemakers, of the agents of subversion.

Look at this one. Camouflaged in the most reassuring way. In the eyes of everybody, of his employees,

126

his employers, his acquaintances, his friends, his neighbors, he was considered a good man, an irreproachable father, entirely devoted to his children... Such well-brought-up, such respectful young people... "I can't say, I've never had any complaint to make of them"... How often people have heard him say that. How often he has been heard congratulating himself at having the good fortune to be the head of a very united family...

Well, would you believe it, in this peaceful home, appointed with exquisite taste, in which he himself grew up with charming parents, with gentle, rosy-cheeked, silver-haired grandparents, among glazed percales and sweet-peas... among so many lovely things, real works of art... there existed a den, a hotbed... the things that went on... Who could have guessed it?... One day a friend overheard, but he couldn't believe his ears, he never spoke of it to anyone, nobody would have understood, any man in his right mind would have known that it was the product of unhealthy imaginings, pure madness... Mere laughter... innocent laughter. Fresh laughter. The kind of laughter you have at that gay, carefree age, at that blessed time, alas so quickly over, when, you remember, a mere nothing was enough to make you laugh, when you had those delightful irrepressible fits of giggling... Well, this character camouflaged as a model father... secretly... through processes known to him alone, succeeded in manufacturing from this laughter miasmas, asphyxiating gases, deadly microbes, a river of rottenness, a sea of muck that would have spread over the entire earth... He was ready to supply all who wanted it with the implement that would let them with impunity make the filth of the entire world gush forth from fresh childish laughter... to sow suspicion... delation... I ask you where we would end up if this were not straightened out? If we didn't move away as from a victim of the pest, if we didn't ban, as a mere measure of hygiene, as a measure of simple security...

He rushes toward them, he attaches himself to them... You know perfectly well that you are lying. However hardened you may be, you can't live in peace if you allow someone to be condemned in your place... You know perfectly well that you provoked everything, everything... as always... slyly...

He lends an ear... Slyly... He sits up astonished... Sly... He hadn't thought of that: sly.

There's something big enough. There's something that can fight against innocents. Against fresh... Sly laughter...

They turn, hesitant, as though abashed, while he gathers his strength, lets go of them, rises and stands in front of them, his arms crossed, with a provocative look... Yes. Sly. That everybody understands. Sly is acceptable. Sly is legal. Sly covers all of that... he makes a broad gesture with his arm that takes them all in, they, the statue set on the table, the friend seated in his easy chair and, up above, on the landing, the door they have left half-open and through which issued... no, not issued, that's not permitted... from which was running, unfurling over them... no, not that either... was running, unfurling has a little touch of dubiousness about it... From which was coming... that's clean, asepticized, perfectly healthy... from which was coming sly laughter. That can be said, can't it? Who doesn't know right away what the word sly means? Who does not use it?

Well, it's like this: their sly laughter produced in me... that too, I can say? That too is allowed? produced—what more normal? —a malaise. What government, what police force, what harsh régime that repressed every attempt at subversion would not authorize an honest man regretfully to state that sly laughter had aroused in him a perfectly natural feeling of malaise?

Who can say anything against that? You see, we are equally divided. On both sides perfectly normal people, citizens who respect the proprieties, observe the customs, the laws. Some assert that it was innocent laughter. And another replies in accordance with the code in force, in the exercise of his rights, that it was sly laughter.

Sly? Is that what you want? Is that all you expect? For someone to state out loud that that laughter was sly? Are you quite sure that this will be all you will have to say? Are you certain that you won't regret it? Don't you think that your appetite is bigger than your stomach? Have you forgotten what happened to you when, imprudently, by dint of sniveling, you ended by getting "mean natures"? Shouldn't that have been a lesson to you, "mean natures"... that amputation from which you thought you would die, for loss of blood?... But "sly" is worse, much more dangerous. "Sly"... think for a moment... sly, we, toward you... We having become a foreign body embedded in your flesh, eating it...

He is staggering, his legs are giving way, his head is reeling, he makes a weak gesture with his hand to stop them... He sees leaning over him their attentive, fond faces... Ah, he's still the same, inflating, boasting, over-estimating his strength, trying to emancipate himself, trying to show his independence...

So you were that frightened of us? And yet you know well that we are not ill-natured... Sly, we, see here, you're joking... You don't really believe it. Where did you get that from?

We, threatening? Dangerous? But how? In what way? Come then, come closer, officer, you can search us, we have no weapons, we had no bad intentions. This gentleman gets ideas into his head. Here are our identity papers. We are from a good family. Very well-brought-up young people. We don't know what got into him. Ask him just to tell you what we did, in what way we behaved badly, how we were lacking in respect.

They approach with an earnest look, pass their fingers over the ears shaped like cartwheels, like seashells, ask questions, listen respectfully to the answers...

So perfectly educated, trained from their earliest years... You have to take them young, even when you have the luck to have been given good specimens from heaven... They stop of their own accord during a walk to point out a tower, a church steeple... A well-adjusted automatic mechanism in them goes off as soon as between the trees, as soon as behind a market square, above the motley brilliance of the overladen fruit and vegetable stands, the delicate grayish form of a church porch is discreetly outlined. They immediately hurry across the sunny square, deaf to the playful cries and calls of the salespeople, and go stand in front of it, heads lifted toward the flattened faces, the defaced limbs of the saints... They turn away with a look of disgust from those hideous stained-glass windows... What degeneracy, what vulgarity... How could that have been allowed? What are the Beaux-Arts for?

That look of connivance with him, that somewhat superior but indulgent little bantering manner they have when in their presence some Boeotian starts to go into ecstasies, when it is obvious that just that, that part here, although not bad, but I think unfortunately that it has been entirely restored... And immediately their eyes leave it, take their distance from it...

Not that it can't ever happen... even to them... let's not exaggerate things, not ask too much... in a moment of inattention or prompted suddenly perhaps by one never knows what bad propensity, what low instinct, to let themselves be attracted... But as soon as they realize that they are slipping, getting into low habits, they pull themselves together... Haven't they acquired immediate self-control, that perfect naturalness by which, at first glance, one recognizes the manners that have become like reflexes, that an accomplished education gives?... The kind that he tried his best to give them... Shouldn't he be satisfied?

But suddenly something is insinuating itself, creeping into him, stinging him... that look of theirs in which at times there is a certain unsteadiness... like a sort of disquiet, of fear... those little gimlets they have which extend, hesitating, fearful... with what circumspection they palpate, settle, coil around, press... But not hard, not the way he does, without really clinging, always ready to detach themselves, a bit limp, a bit flabby, easily led astray... He feels like seizing them and holding them pressed against it by force... there, stay there, since you chose it, since that tempted you, since you like that... What difference does it make for it to have been restored? What difference does it make if it is a copy, since you think it is so fine... If that's what you feel... And they immediately raise their hands to protect themselves... But I don't at all think that's fine, what an idea... I saw that right away... That's not what I was looking at...

There we have it, the brilliant result. That's what we get when we want to erect such a superb edifice... when we cement, repair, mend, choose what doesn't look bad, deserves to be kept, the precious heritage handed down from the beginning of time... when we persist in consolidating, buttressing, raising, improving it... That's what we achieve: a structure which itself is pieced together... an optical illusion... a sham...

We end by no longer recognizing anything, it's impossible to distinguish in them what is genuine from what is fake, where is the original? where is the copy? Even if he takes it apart, piece by piece, examines each one very closely, pitilessly searches everywhere, at the risk, in his rage, but no matter, of tearing off something which was perhaps good, of destroying something which should have been preserved, he doesn't succeed in entirely demolishing them...

He picks his way through the ruins, he is lost in widespread devastation, tripping at every step against formless heaps, aimlessly wandering, hunting...

And suddenly... he gives a start, he tautens, he lifts his head... do you hear them?... something at last that is intact... it's flexible, undulating, vigorous, alive... it's surely theirs... He has had a bad dream, he has not yet destroyed, not damaged, not even affected them, they are strong, made of an excellent unalloyed material which resists all strains... Listen to them, how they are amusing themselves... he raises his head, a beatific expression distends his features...

And the other seated opposite looks at him with friendly eyes... Yes, you see, you agree with me...

there really was nothing to be anxious about... That is very innocent laughter... the kind people indulge in at that age...

He raises his head higher, he is becoming increasingly taut... upstairs, in their quarters, something untoward is afoot... The door opens and a sort of April-fool fish on the end of a line... comes slowly down... He looks... What is that?... He hears little explosions... he sees swaying above his head a sign on which they have written for all to read: Innocent laughter... He seizes it, pulls it off, crumples it and hastily hides it in his pocket... No, not that, not innocent... who do you take me for? I never believed that... The line goes up again... the laughter is exploding in louder peals... And once more on the end of the line a sign is coming down, swaying: Mocking laughter... His avid hand stretches out... Yes, that's it: mocking. Perfect. You hear it: that is mocking laughter. That's obvious and that's fine. At their age, it's a good thing for them to assert themselves vis-à-vis us, I think that is very healthy... The laughter explodes again and again...

The friend is beginning to grow restless in his chair... It may be very healthy, but I think they drag it out a little too long, finally it gets to be exasperating... And the line goes up, comes down again. On the sign, which is swaying back and forth, tickling his friend's skull, is scrawled in enormous letters: Sly laughter... The friend pushes it aside with his hand, but it continues to float about his head, grazes him, goes up, comes down again, finally alights on his bald pate...

he raises his hand, seizes it, looks at it... What is it? Sly... Yes, there is no doubt: sly is the right word... There is just the same—excuse me, it must be acknowledged—in this way of laughing, in this underhanded mockery, since you yourself agree that they intend to mock, something sly...

He looks frightened, what he just said scared him, he is about to retreat... the dramatic reactions provoked by the words "mean natures" must have come into his mind.

But what he sees before him makes him lean forward, both hands clutching the arms of his chair, wide-eyed: a nodding head, a face shining with satisfaction, a beatific smile... Yes, you see I was right, I told you: that is sly laughter. But that word doesn't frighten me. Not in the least. On the contrary. It delights me. When you're being annihilated, when you're being overrun, you have to defend yourself by any means whatsoever. And slyness may be one that is absolutely necessary. Very effective. Sly suits me. It suits me for these children to be sly, for them to be what they want to be, for them to be just anything whatsoever, provided they are what they are. Provided they exist... really... They can assert themselves against me if necessary, I accept that, I want it... they can hurt me, they can trample me underfoot, if that can be beneficial to them, they can kill me, in fact...

The laughter ceases. The signs go up again. And they themselves come down, come up to him... How wild you look... They caress his head, they hand him a handkerchief... Here, I hate to see you like that... You're looking for something with which to torture, to wound yourself... What have you gone and dug up now? What does that mean, what can possibly be the sense for us of: Sly. Mocking. Innocent?... Innocent, you know very well, was no better. How could you think that these ordinary words, used by other people, by outsiders... these words taken from their word-books, from their dictionaries...

That's true, they are right, how could these old sclerotic words retain, enclose the fluid, fluctuating thing that circulates among us, in constant transformation, spreading out in every direction, that no boundary can stop... that is ours, ours alone... What outside word can set things right between us, separate or bring us together?... You know perfectly well that here, between us, all these words... We used them for fun. In play...

He feels their fresh firm cheeks against his, he breathes in the milk-and-honey odor of their skin, the young sap that rises from them and flows into him... he tears himself away from them, pushes them away... No, leave me alone. No, that must not happen. No fusion... We must keep our distance. I would only hinder you, weigh upon you... A heavyweight. A dead weight. And in any case, nature knows best, the time will come, it's not so far off...

They lay their smooth palms on his mouth... Hush, don't talk about that... You know very well that we can't stand it... —All right, all right, I won't say anything... But you're tickling me... He shakes his head with feigned grumpiness... leave me alone, what are you up to? He feels their delicate fingers against his neck... —You've let it grow too long again... I absolutely must cut it for you... He does that out of vanity, you know how he is. He thinks he's handsomer like that... He tosses his head, he laughs... —You are silly...

And suddenly, it can't be helped, he can't stop it, a joyous impulse makes him lean over the table, seize the animal, hold it out to them... Here, take this. Take it with you. In any case, it will be yours. And I don't want it any more. Really? I'm not attached to it, I'm not attached to anything, you know that very well, except to that pack... jerking his head in their direction... to those little morons... I wonder why, really... Well, what are you waiting for? Don't you want it?

They don't budge, they have an embarrassed look... —But you're not serious? For us? You'll miss it... —I tell you, I don't care... Besides, I know...

She holds out her arms, she takes the animal in both hands, she presses it to her... —You know that I'll watch over it, I'll take good care of it, you'll come to visit it... That way, at least... she shakes her finger, she gives him a teasing smile... you'll come up to see us more often, perhaps, you big bad wolf...

Where on earth is it, for God's sake? It was there, I put it aside... but they took possession of it as usual, to look up goodness knows what, goodness knows what can interest them... without asking him, they think they can do anything they like, they take everything he has...

He climbs the stairs, waits in front of the door, his hand on the knob... It would be better to go back down again, give up, not see, not confront... Not know it... May this hour pass... He hasn't the heart... But what are these fits of weakness, of cowardice... as though anything about them could still surprise him... after all he's not going to wait for them to come out to ask them... he must have it now... he turns the knob, suddenly he opens the door... And of course... in the midst of the disorder, of records lying about everywhere, of magazines all over the floor, scattered clothing... well, well, there it is, I knew it. No doubt about it, you are hopeless. Naturally you are the ones who took it... —What? What did we take?... He stoops, picks it up. —You could see however that it's this week's issue... I hardly had time to glance at it... How many times have I asked you... But it is as if I were talking to myself... —Okay, I promise you I won't do it again, I thought you had already read it, it had been lying around for several days... But don't leave right away, sit down for a minute... He gives a sigh... —Where?... in this disorder... They dance attendance on him, they straighten up, they put the records, the picture-books, in piles to make room on the divan, and he drops down on it... —Wait, we'll

138

give you a cushion... there... you'll be more com-
fortable... He sits back still grumbling a little and
they gather about him, crouching on piles of news-
papers, seated cross-legged on the carpet.

His gaze, as though listless, as though seeing nothing,
skims over the walls, over the furniture... dwells for
a second on the chest... turns aside... Yes, it is still
there, he has located the dark mass in the place where
he had helped put it, stepping back, coming closer to
make sure that it would be well lighted by the light
from the window... As he listens to them, as he talks
with them, he grazes it again with an absent glance...
piles of letters, postcards, prospectuses partly hide it,
resting against its muzzle, against its flank... And on
its back there is a sort of protuberance... Prudently,
as though wandering at random, his gaze returns to it...
It looks like one of those seats that domesticated ele-
phants are made to carry, only the canopy is missing...
He tries to talk as though nothing were wrong, but
his voice has a hollow, unreal sound... a ghost's
voice... It is a dark-colored cup-shaped object... his
vacant gaze passes over it... he recognizes it... it is
a giant oyster shell... full to the brim probably with
cigarette butts, ashes, and the animal now serves it as
a support... or in all probability... it would be a
mistake to attribute such a deliberate motive, such a
well-defined project to them... they simply forgot that
they had put it there in a moment of inattention, to
make room, or else to raise it to the level of a hand
holding a cigarette, which was straining, swaying, me-
chanically looking for a hollow object into which to

139

shake the ash... Shyly, timorously he looks else-where...

Above all, not let them see anything, play dead... they can touch him as much as they want, turn him over and over, he is indifferent, blind, passive...

But how could these childish tricks fool them? From the very moment he came in, the moment he sat down, in spite of his listless look, his absent-minded air, they knew that he had seen everything... they perceive each tiny wave, each eddy of what wells up in him and which he tries his best to hold back... But already he can't stand it any longer, he rises, he heads directly for it... in a second he's going to hold out his arm, with the back of his hand sweep away the post-cards, the ash-tray, make it roll across the floor in a deafening din... in the roar of the wave that through the crack he will open, savagely chipping the glazed surface, is going to gush forth, swell, break over them, over him, drag them along clinging to one another, suffocated, asphyxiated... they curl up, they hide their heads in their hands... And then, hearing nothing, they risk a peek and see him standing near the chest, his hand outstretched toward the animal's back, putting out his cigarette in the ash-tray...

They grow restless, jostle, knock against one an-other... Did you see him? Is it possible? What's happening? They can't believe it... This is complete surrender, bag and baggage, it is renunciation, it is abandonment... He has finally understood that all he can do now is to submit, to accept what is ineluctable... to destroy within himself every stray impulse of revolt, the slightest residue of hope... his hand lingers, crushing the cigarette-end hard against the bottom of the ash-tray, his fingers triturate it, scatter the tobacco, roll the paper into a wad...

Then he turns round. He opens his jacket, puts his hands in his trousers' pockets and faces them, head high, chest out... In his eyes there is a strange, unusual expression of indifference, of benevolent distance... It's a mistake, you know, to treat this poor animal like that... You ought really to take care of it. It's a rather rare specimen, and it's worth its weight in gold... They feel pressed on their faces the expression of a certain worthy lady whom he had often shown them—she is part of his collection—and who, standing in front of a canvas in the atelier of a famous painter, asked: And that, *maître,* what does that represent? and got the insolent reply: That, Madam? that represents three hundred thousand francs... They pull off that ludicrous mask, they show their faces over which flickers the ghost of a smile...

—Why are you smiling? You don't believe me? As for me, you know what I say about it is for you... —Yes, of course we believe you... They nod their heads, rigged out this time with faces congealed by the sad, detached seriousness suited to dark-garbed heirs, seated about a notary's table, looking through his papers... Let's see, there's still this collection piece... The experts estimate it very highly...

She is the first to bestir herself, she rises, runs toward the chest, takes the ash-tray in her hand and sets it beside the animal... —I wonder who put that there...

141

No matter how often I tell them... She doesn't touch the postcards, they are more like a protection... You see you should never have given it to us... You know very well what we are like... You know us... You would do better to take it back... The others, as though awakened, sit up straight, tear themselves away from the sinister desk, from the walls covered with dusty files, escape, emerge into the light, the air of the out-of-doors... —She's right. You know what you ought to do really to set your mind at rest?... you ought to make a gift of it to a museum... Why not to the Louvre? Didn't you tell us that they were going to open a room for pre-Columbian art? The Louvre, that would be perfect.

But what's the matter? What's wrong?... Why don't you answer, say something... You don't want to? Not in the Louvre? Not in a museum? Is that it? You prefer for us to keep it? Is that what you want? Say something... You prefer that? You would like us to put it in a glass case, under lock and key?... He nods his head weakly... No, he doesn't want... not in a glass case... not kept out of piety, of pity... It's from where, that statue? Oh, I don't know, I've always seen it here, a family heirloom... I believe it belonged to one of my grandfathers... But don't get so upset, nothing will be done against your will... you see very well that it would be better off there... Where would it be better off, come now, let's be reasonable, than in a museum? Better cared for, better appreciated? Really, it's astonishing... You who like museums so much, eh? You who have passed the better part of your time in them... don't blush... of your free time, I mean... and when I say "better," I don't mean to denigrate... I say "better" the way you say better weather, better times... bright, if you want... Ah, you see, he's smiling, he understands...

Where would it be more in its element than in a beautiful sumptuous museum, a palace?... That's why we thought of the Louvre... Those splendid rooms, you remember, those stretches of shining inlaid floors, those high windows that frame the gardens... and those little rooms at the top, intimate as little chapels, propitious for meditation, for prayer... That's where it would be best off, no doubt, if they will accept to put it there... Imagine it among the donations, the valuable acquisitions, protected like the one you liked so much, near the window, in its glass cube... a soft light falling across its flank...

He curls up, he raises his hand as though to protect himself... as though to beg them... What is the matter with you?... No, what is the good in insisting? he shakes his head... No, he doesn't want... then what do you want? You must say it, make up your mind... and above all don't think that it's because we want to get rid of it... the little old man whose children want to put him in a "home" must not think, above all... you know that for us, it's not to our interest, for us it's rather a sacrifice... everything we say about it is for you, you know... you must make up your mind instead of worrying... He nods approval, his mouth stretches in a nice toothless smile... I'll do as you like. In any case it will soon be up to you to decide...

It's touching that they should be so anxious... that shows lots of consideration... You see how they can exasperate me at times... as, for instance, with their stupid little titters... But I must be fair, I shouldn't complain... In reality they are very nice with me... Few people today can say as much... You can say what you want, they are nice children... You see that thing over there... which you like so much, I wanted to let them have it, well they themselves suggested, they even insisted, that I should make a gift of it to a museum... Yes, I'm lucky. Personally, you see, I would have liked for them to keep it for themselves... After all, to live with things like that does make a difference... But what's the use in going against their wishes, don't you agree? Each one of us is free to find happiness where he will... I accepted. There are people for whom it will give moments... even for them, does one ever know... the things that constantly surround us, we end up by not seeing them anymore... Even they, one day, who knows?

Is it really possible? There, in the line waiting in front of the ticket window, that head... He is pushing his way forward, jostling the other people... What is he doing? you don't belong there... There are always boors who try to get ahead of everybody else... No, I just wanted to see... just a second... excuse me...

144

No, of course, that was too good... But those peals of laughter behind him... he turns around... And all his solitude, his abandon, all his distress are spread over these unknown faces, flow back to him from that icy laughter... But what's the matter? What happened? It's that little old man back there, in the line, he felt faint... There... do you feel better? Yes, it's nothing... There now. It's over...

What is the matter with you? You look very sad, you look woebegone... —No, not at all... Of course, I would have preferred for you to keep it, but I'm wrong, I know that... One shouldn't be egoistical... It's better like that... Others will take advantage of it... They caress his head, they smile at him... He raises toward them a humble glance, the timid, guilty glance of a child... But you too, isn't that so? That will give you pleasure perhaps, after all, from time to time?... —Of course it will, you know that...

—Let's see, where did you say it is? You don't remember? I haven't set foot in here for ages... —Nor have I, what do you think... In any case, it couldn't be in this section... If we have time, later we can take advantage of the occasion... —It's incredible, the things you can see, and re-see... things you would never have thought of... when you are showing Paris to friends from the provinces, from abroad... If I were to tell you that without you I would never have gone to Saint-Denis to see the tombs of the Kings of France... I would never have gone back to Notre-Dame—and yet I pass in front of it every day—to see the stained-glass windows. And as for the Louvre...

How moving these people are, what a scream they are when they stop dumbfounded, congealed... when they nudge one another, whisper, quite astonished, amused, flattered to have recognized from a distance... as though at a first night performance they recognized in flesh and blood the celebrities whose photographs they have seen on the front pages of magazines... Oh, look over there... Leonardo da Vinci's Saint-Jean-Baptiste... And there... Why, it's the Outdoor Concert! And over here, come and look... Raphaël... Jeanne of Aragon... It makes you feel like looking elsewhere, moving away... And yet there's no danger, no chance that you'll meet friends here, unless they too, poor dears... unless they too are the victims of one of these boring stints...

—I'm sorry to hurry you but I think it's time to leave... However, just one moment... We can go out that way, it's just as close... There must be near here, I think, in one of the little rooms on the right... a pre-Columbian statue... it belonged to our family... Why, there it is, here, over there, next to the window...

They come closer and stand before it in reverent silence. The friends lean over and respectfully read the inscription... —You remember when one of us thoughtlessly said that it was a Cretan sculpture? What a crime! My father was ready to kill her... he raises his head... Poor Papa... But you know if we want to see everything... And I feel sure that you don't dare tell us all your plans... I bet we'll have to go to the Pantheon, make a pilgrimage to Père-Lachaise... You see, we've still got plenty to do...

Their laughter is coming in peals... Carefree laughter. Innocent laughter. Laughter for no one. Laughter in space. Their voices make a confused noise which grows weaker, fades away...

It is as though a door upstairs were closing... And then, nothing.

COLEMAN DOWELL SERIES

The Coleman Dowell Series is made possible through a generous contribution by an anonymous donor. This endowed contribution allows Dalkey Archive Press to publish one book a year in this series.

Born in Kentucky in 1925, Coleman Dowell moved to New York in 1950 to work in theater and television as a playwright and composer/lyricist, but by age forty turned to writing fiction. His works include *One of the Children Is Crying* (1968), *Mrs. October Was Here* (1974), *Island People* (1976), *Too Much Flesh and Jabez* (1977), and *White on Black on White* (1983). After his death in 1985, *The Houses of Children: Collected Stories* was published in 1987, and his memoir about his theatrical years, *A Star-Bright Lie,* was published in 1993.

Since his death, a number of his books have been reissued in the United States, as well as translated for publication in other countries.

SELECTED DALKEY ARCHIVE PAPERBACKS

PIERRE ALBERT-BIROT, *Grabinoulor.*
YUZ ALESHKOVSKY, *Kangaroo.*
FELIPE ALFAU, *Chromos.*
   Locos.
   Sentimental Songs.
IVAN ÂNGELO, *The Celebration.*
   The Tower of Glass.
ALAN ANSEN, *Contact Highs: Selected Poems 1957-1987.*
DAVID ANTIN, *Talking.*
DJUNA BARNES, *Ladies Almanack.*
   Ryder.
JOHN BARTH, *LETTERS.*
   Sabbatical.
ANDREI BITOV, *Pushkin House.*
LOUIS PAUL BOON, *Chapel Road.*
ROGER BOYLAN, *Killoyle.*
IGNÁCIO DE LOYOLA BRANDÃO, *Zero.*
CHRISTINE BROOKE-ROSE, *Amalgamemnon.*
BRIGID BROPHY, *In Transit.*
MEREDITH BROSNAN, *Mr. Dynamite.*
GERALD L. BRUNS,
   Modern Poetry and the Idea of Language.
GABRIELLE BURTON, *Heartbreak Hotel.*
MICHEL BUTOR, *Mobile.*
   Portrait of the Artist as a Young Ape.
JULIETA CAMPOS, *The Fear of Losing Eurydice.*
ANNE CARSON, *Eros the Bittersweet.*
CAMILO JOSÉ CELA, *The Family of Pascual Duarte.*
   The Hive.
LOUIS-FERDINAND CÉLINE, *Castle to Castle.*
   London Bridge.
   North.
   Rigadoon.
HUGO CHARTERIS, *The Tide Is Right.*
JEROME CHARYN, *The Tar Baby.*
MARC CHOLODENKO, *Mordechai Schamz.*
EMILY HOLMES COLEMAN, *The Shutter of Snow.*
ROBERT COOVER, *A Night at the Movies.*
STANLEY CRAWFORD, *Some Instructions to My Wife.*
ROBERT CREELEY, *Collected Prose.*
RENÉ CREVEL, *Putting My Foot in It.*
RALPH CUSACK, *Cadenza.*
SUSAN DAITCH, *L.C.*
   Storytown.
NIGEL DENNIS, *Cards of Identity.*
PETER DIMOCK,
   A Short Rhetoric for Leaving the Family.
ARIEL DORFMAN, *Konfidenz.*
COLEMAN DOWELL, *The Houses of Children.*
   Island People.
   Too Much Flesh and Jabez.
RIKKI DUCORNET, *The Complete Butcher's Tales.*
   The Fountains of Neptune.
   The Jade Cabinet.
   Phosphor in Dreamland.
   The Stain.
WILLIAM EASTLAKE, *The Bamboo Bed.*
   Castle Keep.
   Lyric of the Circle Heart.
JEAN ECHENOZ, *Chopin's Move.*
STANLEY ELKIN, *A Bad Man.*
   Boswell: A Modern Comedy.
   Criers and Kibitzers, Kibitzers and Criers.
   The Dick Gibson Show.
   The Franchiser.

   George Mills.
   The Living End.
   The MacGuffin.
   The Magic Kingdom.
   Mrs. Ted Bliss.
   The Rabbi of Lud.
   Van Gogh's Room at Arles.
ANNIE ERNAUX, *Cleaned Out.*
LAUREN FAIRBANKS, *Muzzle Thyself.*
   Sister Carrie.
LESLIE A. FIEDLER,
   Love and Death in the American Novel.
FORD MADOX FORD, *The March of Literature.*
CARLOS FUENTES, *Terra Nostra.*
   Where the Air Is Clear.
JANICE GALLOWAY, *Foreign Parts.*
   The Trick Is to Keep Breathing.
WILLIAM H. GASS, *The Tunnel.*
   Willie Masters' Lonesome Wife.
ETIENNE GILSON, *The Arts of the Beautiful.*
   Forms and Substances in the Arts.
C. S. GISCOMBE, *Giscome Road.*
   Here.
DOUGLAS GLOVER, *Bad News of the Heart.*
KAREN ELIZABETH GORDON, *The Red Shoes.*
PATRICK GRAINVILLE, *The Cave of Heaven.*
HENRY GREEN, *Blindness.*
   Concluding.
   Doting.
   Nothing.
JIŘÍ GRUŠA, *The Questionnaire.*
JOHN HAWKES, *Whistlejacket.*
AIDAN HIGGINS, *A Bestiary.*
   Flotsam and Jetsam.
   Langrishe, Go Down.
ALDOUS HUXLEY, *Antic Hay.*
   Crome Yellow.
   Point Counter Point.
   Those Barren Leaves.
   Time Must Have a Stop.
MIKHAIL IOSSEL AND JEFF PARKER, EDS.,
   Amerika: Contemporary Russians View the
   United States.
GERT JONKE, *Geometric Regional Novel.*
JACQUES JOUET, *Mountain R.*
DANILO KIŠ, *Garden, Ashes.*
   A Tomb for Boris Davidovich.
TADEUSZ KONWICKI, *A Minor Apocalypse.*
   The Polish Complex.
ELAINE KRAF, *The Princess of 72nd Street.*
JIM KRUSOE, *Iceland.*
EWA KURYLUK, *Century 21.*
VIOLETTE LEDUC, *La Bâtarde.*
DEBORAH LEVY, *Billy and Girl.*
   Pillow Talk in Europe and Other Places.
JOSÉ LEZAMA LIMA, *Paradiso.*
OSMAN LINS, *Avalovara.*
   The Queen of the Prisons of Greece.
ALF MAC LOCHLAINN, *The Corpus in the Library.*
   Out of Focus.
RON LOEWINSOHN, *Magnetic Field(s).*
D. KEITH MANO, *Take Five.*
BEN MARCUS, *The Age of Wire and String.*
WALLACE MARKFIELD, *Teitlebaum's Window.*
   To an Early Grave.

FOR A FULL LIST OF PUBLICATIONS, VISIT:
www.dalkeyarchive.com

SELECTED DALKEY ARCHIVE PAPERBACKS

FOR A FULL LIST OF PUBLICATIONS, VISIT:
www.dalkeyarchive.com